THE CHILDREN

Carolina Sanín

THE CHILDREN

Translated from the Spanish by
Nick Caistor

MACLEHOSE PRESS
QUERCUS · LONDON

First published in the Spanish language as *Los niños* by Laguna Libros, SAS, in Barcelona, 2014
First published in Great Britain in 2017 by
MacLehose Press
An imprint of Quercus Publishing Ltd
Carmelite House
50 Victoria Embankment
London EC4Y 0DZ

An Hachette UK company

A CIP catalogue record for this book is available
from the British Library.

ISBN (HB) 978 0 85705 586 6
ISBN (Ebook) 978 0 85705 585 9

10 9 8 7 6 5 4 3 2 1

Designed and typeset in Haarlemmer by Lbanus Press, Marlborough
Printed and bound in Great Britain by Clays Ltd, St Ives plc

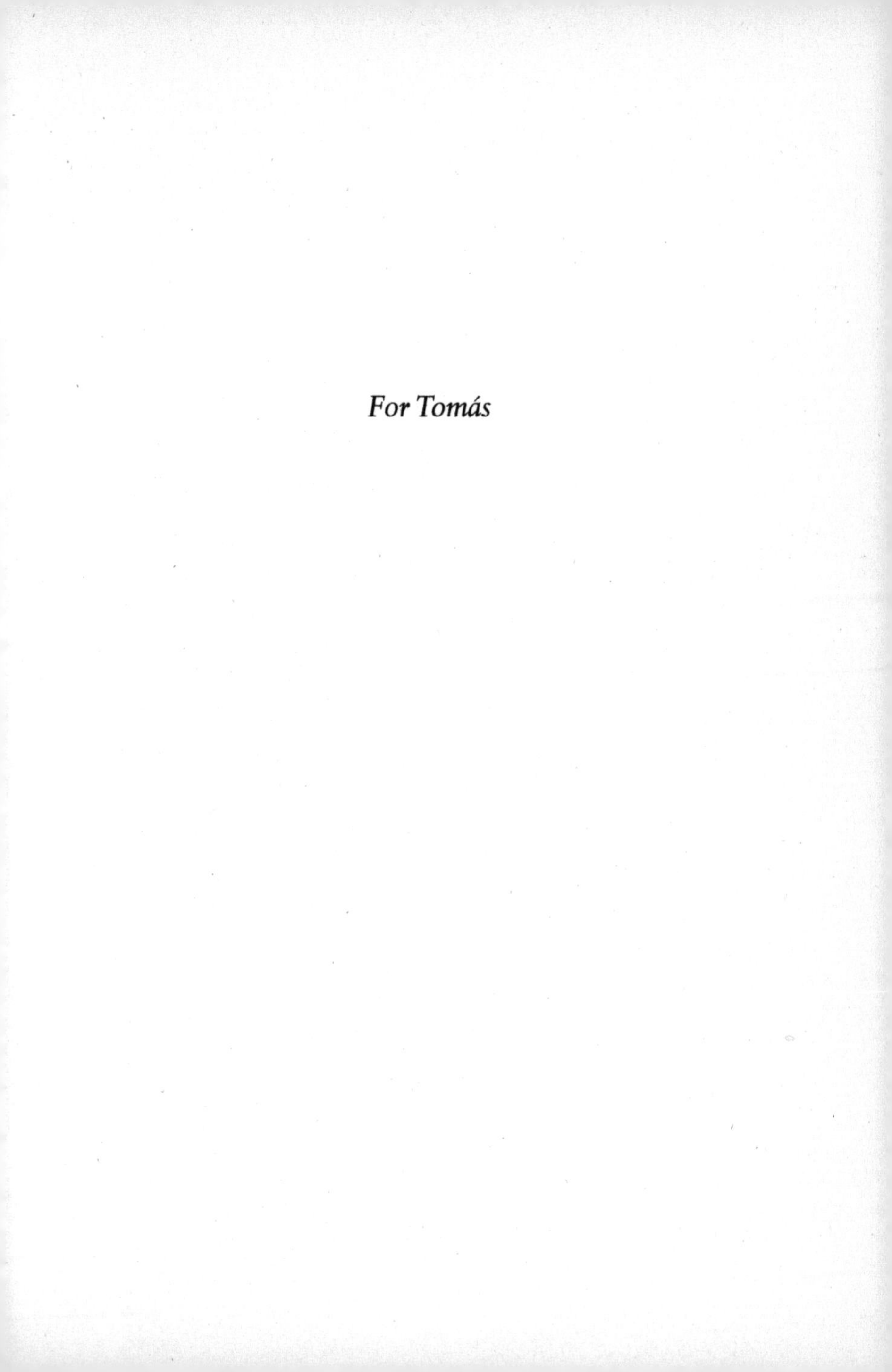

For Tomás

Gloria: I asked you once if I could be your mother. You didn't want that.

Phil: Do you want to be my mother? You could be my mother. I don't have any mother. No more mother. So you could be my mother. Why would you want to be my mother?

Gloria: I don't know. Just want to clear things up.

Phil: You're my mother. You're my father. You're my whole family. You're even my friend, Gloria. You're my girlfriend, too.

JOHN CASSAVETES, *Gloria*

I

I

Laura Romero heard that the woman who watched the cars outside the supermarket was offering her a child. She heard her say: *I'll keep the child for you.* But Laura was not sure whether the woman really did watch the cars. She knew that when she had finished her shopping, she gave her some coins as if to pay her, and that her car had never gone missing. Maybe that was because she only left it there during daylight and when there were lots of people about, but it was also possible that the woman had some influence over the car thieves. That she was their mother, for example.

Laura used to leave the Renault in the car park outside the Olímpica, which was the name of the supermarket. The woman would see her arrive and nod, or if she was close enough, say to her: *I'll keep an eye on it for you.* Laura would enter the supermarket, do her shopping, come out and put the coins in the woman's hand. The thought crossed her mind that perhaps she was paying so as not to be as battered-looking as the woman, with a face ruined from standing out in the open the whole day long.

She looked as if she had been close to death at some point in her life. She did not look ill so much as cured in the distant past. It might have been that she did not sleep or had walked from a long way away, so far it seemed she had not arrived yet. Were those scars or stains on her face? They looked like the maps of islands.

Laura lived a few blocks from the Olímpica, so she often walked there, making the most of the opportunity to take her dog Brus for a walk. She left him tied to the supermarket rail, and sometimes when she came out she bumped into a passer-by who had stopped to admire him, and was saying what a beautiful dog, how wonderful, and what breed is he?

Greyhounds were not common in Bogotá. Some people thought he was just a skinny example of a breed they did know who had been unlucky enough to fall into the hands of a bad owner. One day in Simón Bolívar park, she had to put up with someone shouting at her: *Why don't you feed him, you fat cow?* Laura did not think she was fat, although she was not as sleek as the greyhound, nor as she herself had been twenty years earlier. She was dark-skinned, with long, wavy hair, which had more white in it than she could see in the mirror. When she got the child and their story began, those who knew her had been saying for a decade already: *She used to be a great beauty.*

Whenever a stranger asked her the dog's name, Laura gave a different answer: Phoenix, Shiny, Thorny, Crow, Hummingbird. By doing this she thought she was protecting him: that it was less likely someone would snatch him from the supermarket entrance or anywhere else. If they called out: *Soul!* or *Spike!* or *Thistle!* he would not look in their direction. Anyone who wanted to steal him would have to use force. They might succeed in the end and take him, but they would not have his real name, which would still belong to her.

The woman who watched the cars had on several occasions offered to look after the dog while Laura was shopping, but she always said no, thank you, he preferred to wait for her on his own at the entrance.

Brus was the colour of pale sand. His long, deceptively trusting face made him look like the woman who kept an eye on the cars.

All this is leading up to the afternoon when Laura heard the woman say: *I'll keep the child for you.*

Laura was bending down to tie the dog up in the supermarket entrance when she sensed someone whispering behind her. She thought it sounded like a voice with no feet to hold it up, carry it along or make it come to a halt, but when she turned round, there the woman was. Until that moment, all she had ever heard her say was: *I'll watch it for you*, which always sounded halfway between asking her for something and apologising. The voice talking about the child sounded different, as if it had been shaken free of its roots, not like the voices of the living, who talk as they grow.

"What did you say?"

"I'll keep the child for you," the woman said, and as she repeated it, the voice stepped down a rung of the imaginary ladder Laura had created for it.

The woman raised her hand to point to the dog and explained she was offering to take it outside while his owner was doing the shopping.

Laura refused as usual, and went inside the Olímpica. She had a pencil and a written list in her hand. She read a word on the list, found the corresponding item on the shelf, put it in her basket and then crossed out the word. Each time she looked at the piece of paper she also read something that was not written down.

Oil. The woman offered me a child. She wanted to give me one of her children, but my reaction made her hesitate, and to cover up she tried to make me think she was calling Brus a "child".

Onion. The woman didn't want to get rid of her child. If

I thought she wanted to give him to me, that's because I wanted to have him.

Parsley. The woman called Brus a "child" because she herself changed a child into Brus by a spell before he became my dog.

Eggs. Maybe when I give my dog the names of animals, plants and other things I am creating a recipe to bewitch him.

Pepper. Perhaps she watches the cars outside the supermarket simply by looking at them, casting a spell on them.

Laura came out of the supermarket, looked for the woman and gave her the same coins she always gave her. Or rather, she gave her some more coins that were added to the ones she had previously given her. Although of course it was possible they were the same ones: perhaps at the end of the day the woman bought a loaf of bread with them in the supermarket, and the next day the cashier gave them back to Laura as change from the banknote she used to buy her shopping with.

Laura went back to her apartment. She put the list away in the cutlery drawer in the kitchen, and prepared an omelette with the ingredients she had just bought. She never bought salt, because she had plenty of that. She kept a big bag of it in the maid's room, where there was no maid. Her mother's family were the owners of a salt mine in the mountains, so she received a bag of salt each month, plus a cheque for her share of the profits, together with that of her brother and her mother, who had given her part to Laura whilst she was still alive.

She did not go back to the Olímpica the following day because she had prepared enough omelettes to eat three times daily for the next two days. When she went back on the third morning, walking there with Brus, the woman who usually kept an eye on the cars was not there. Someone younger had taken her place, with a boy and a girl who followed her across the car park like a pair of ducklings. All three of them looked clean and well dressed. The woman was wearing high-heeled ankle boots and a striped cotton suit. She had blonde hair in a braided bun, and nobody would have thought she was there to look after cars or dogs. As the other woman had done on the previous occasion, she came over as Laura bent down to tie the leash to the rail.

"I'll keep your dog," she said.

Laura looked up and was about to say no, thank you, when the other woman asked if she *spoke languages*. She said her little brother and sister didn't speak Spanish and had no-one they could ask what they wanted to know. So could she please talk to them.

The children stepped forward. They had realised the dog was a greyhound. They asked in English if he had ever raced, if she had rescued him from a dog track or had him since he was a puppy. If she had won him in a bet. And please, for the love of God, would she give him to them. And what was his name.

As they talked they held out their hands, palms upward, as if expecting her to give them some change. Laura was unable to invent a name for Brus, and went back home with him without going into the supermarket. She pushed her way along, driven on by the fear these strangers and their strange chorus had produced in her.

For the next two days, she did not buy any food, and she did not eat. At breakfast-time she drove through the Olímpica's tarmac lot to see whether the clean beggars were still there. When she caught a glimpse of the blonde woman she felt frightened again, and kept on going. It was only on the third day, when the other, haggard woman had returned to her post in the car park, that Laura felt able to go into the supermarket once more.

Although the child who arrived a month later apparently had nothing to do with any of this, it was imprinted on Laura's mind that she had asked for him the afternoon she had thought the woman who watched the cars was offering her a child.

Even though the boy who arrived said he was six and a

half, Laura was persuaded in her own mind that he had been conceived the same evening that she had summoned him as she prepared the omelette with the ingredients she had bought in the Olímpica.

She was also convinced that, on the third day after he was conceived, the blonde woman with a foreign little brother and sister had breathed a breath so that the heart of the child whose name was Fidel began to beat.

It was as if for Laura memory, desire and promise were one and the same, something that yet was different from the other three.

2

Four weeks passed until the evening that Laura thought of as the day of the birth of Fidel.

She had boarded a bus to return home from work, which was somewhere unsuitable for travelling to by car. She worked in the Santa Ana district, in the house of an elderly couple, where she cleaned and did the housework three times a week – Monday, Wednesday and Friday – for six hours each day. She would have been at a loss to explain why she worked as a cleaner when she had no need to. She could give some reasons, but would they be the real ones? And if they were real, would they not demonstrate that she did need that job after all? She preferred to tell herself that everything else she had done in her life until then – reading books, looking at paintings, watching films and T.V. programmes, doing voice-overs for furniture advertisements and for the speaking clock on the telephone – had allowed her to gain some idea of how a home should be, and that this idea permitted her to do a good job cleaning the tiles in the shower, cooking, making the bed and bleaching the sheets with chlorine until they had holes in them. What else could she have tried her hand at? Few tasks seemed to her better than looking after a house and making it shine.

If she had gone to work in her car, her employers would have realised she was not doing it for the money they paid her, and instead of assuming she was doing it because she was good at it, would have thought she was doing it for fun, or to suffer, or to spy on them. They would no longer have thought they could give her orders and would have sacked her on the spot, or would have been interested in her story, and she would have ended up having to tell them about the income she received from her family's salt mine. She would have had to admit she lived on money that came from the past and would have felt awkward. Also, her employers would have discovered they were distant relatives of hers, and that would have been another reason to get rid of her.

And so she came and went by bus. She arrived at eight in the morning and left at two in the afternoon. And that Friday afternoon, when she was coming back from work having stayed on at the last minute to darn one of the old man's jerseys, a man boarded the bus to sell and threaten. Laura, who was reading *Moby-Dick*, looked up from her book. The man blocked the aisle facing the passengers, and said:

Good day, ladies and gentlemen, I wish you a good day. First of all, I should like to thank all those of you who responded to my greeting: you are truly refined, humane people. I was once in the grip of vice. I consumed herbal and artificial drugs, stole whatever I could lay my hands on, and beat my children, a little boy aged nine, who's a tremendous Don Juan, and his two-year-old baby sister, who is a real glutton and very expensive, eating us out of house and home, and I stabbed a policeman and held up buses like a pirate at sea. But for three months now I've kept on the straight and narrow and instead I've been selling this product I am offering you today and which I shall now proceed to reference. It is a delicious jam that comes in practical plastic bags. There are milk and raspberry flavours – raspberries are a kind of foreign fruit. It also comes in a special flavour. Jam consists principally of a substance, sweet or otherwise, that is spread on bread. Bread, to be precise, is one of the most important foodstuffs in the world, and by good fortune it is also for sale here today in this famous means of transport. To swallow it you need no more than pure water or any other drinkable liquid. With this jam, bread is more nutritious and delicious, both for boys and girls and for their mamás and papás. Today I am offering the jam at a specially discounted price, because with the purchase of two buns it will be at half the usual rate. In addition, the bag or bladder it comes in is completely without charge, and can be reused for storing provisions, for transporting jewels, for storing pencils, as a goldfish bowl, or to throw up in should the bus journey upset any consumer's stomach. As you can see, in this other hand I am holding a knife that has been properly sharpened, which can be used to spread the jam or for many other tasks. The knife is not for sale, as it is the humble tool of my trade.

With the switchblade in one hand and the box containing the bags of jam and buns in the other, the vendor passed down the aisle looking for purchasers. Laura bought a bun because she did not dare not to, either to let it grow mouldy or to measure the passage of time by how hard it became, or to throw it from her balcony into the rubbish bin out in the street. She imagined the mugger's children, the boy and girl who got beaten and who ate too much, chased the girls and kept pencils and goldfish in the plastic bags for the jam. The next night she found Fidel. Much later on she decided that while she was listening to this spiel on the bus, Fidel was being born; that the bus journey had taken place six and a half years before the day that actually followed it, and nine months after the day she had misunderstood the woman who kept an eye on the cars in the Olímpica, which was the day when Fidel had been wished for.

Sometimes, while she was cleaning the old couple's

house, Laura built another house in the future and in her memory. She put three bedrooms at the back. Between the dining room and the bedrooms she planted a garden with a curving stream that carried along with it ordinary stones and precious stones. The ordinary ones were so polished they looked as if they were made of steel, and the precious ones were cut so that they sparkled like lights. In the middle of the garden Laura put a bridge, and at the edge of the endlessly rushing water she laid out a beach where the fish could spawn. After laying their eggs in the morning, some of the fish stayed on land until two in the afternoon so as to explore the island, the bridge, the garden and the entire house. Some of them had four legs, like donkeys and horses strong enough for long journeys; others were like oxen, and could pull almost anything, while others still were like lions or foxes in the shape of dogs, and were fleeter of foot than any other animal in the world. Laura imagined that the bedrooms had wallpaper patterned with forest scenes, and furniture painted with birds flying in the painted sky. They were not birds that had ever appeared on earth, and yet they had already changed their plumage a hundred thousand times. The ceilings were domes of sapphire and lapis lazuli, with crystals like fireflies encrusted in them. In the kitchen there was a big onyx table that was black earth freshly ploughed for a new crop. Laura constructed this house to imitate a place and realm she had read of in an ancient book, and it was not so much that she wanted it for herself but so that she could work in two places at the same time.

3

Brus became aware of Fidel's existence before she did. It was shortly before midnight on Saturday, and Laura had just filled the hot-water bottle she took to bed with her. The dog began to bark and then to howl, and in between could be heard sobs that seemed to have been learned by heart, as if they came from a child who knows he is too big to still be crying like that. Laura tilted her head the way Brus did when she asked him something, and realised that the sound was coming from the street, on the right-hand side of the building as you looked out. She went onto the balcony. A boy was looking up from the pavement, three storeys down. As soon as he saw her appear, he stopped crying.

"I'm going down," Laura told the dog, who had hidden behind the sofa and was still howling.

The boy had a shaven head and big eyes. There was so much black emptiness in his gaze that it seemed as though his face had interrupted the night and the night had begun again in his look. He was neither dark nor fair. He seemed to be both, white in the light from the street lamp, and dark from daytime sun. He was wearing inadequate clothing for the cold Bogotá night: a very short pair of shorts, with curved hems and a white stripe, flip-flops and a sleeveless T-shirt with a picture on it of Naranjito, the mascot of a football World Cup from almost thirty years previously.

Laura asked him if he was looking for someone in the building. She told him to wait a minute and not to go away. She went back up to her apartment and came down again with a blanket that she wrapped round his shoulders. She thought about going up again to fetch him something to eat and a glass of water, but instead took him upstairs with her.

"I couldn't get in," the boy said in the lift.

When he heard someone arriving, Brus did not rush to the door.

Laura asked the boy if he was lost. What his name was. If he wanted her to take him somewhere.

He said something very quietly, and she bent down in order to hear him if he repeated it. Instead of that he gave her a quick peck on the ear, more in the air than actually on her skin.

Laura went into the kitchen with the boy at her heels. She

tore off a piece of the bread from the day before, the bread from the bus, and gave it to him. He swallowed it without even chewing, and she gave him the rest of the loaf. The dog appeared with his head hung low and his muzzle extended, wagging his tail between his legs. Laura said his name was Brus. The boy took two steps backwards, and Brus slunk away, his tail now still.

Laura called the police. She said she had found someone who was lost.

"Didn't you call last night about the same thing?" asked the operator.

She said she had not.

"It's that woman about the missing person," whispered the operator to someone who must have been sitting beside her in the police station, and who asked:

"Didn't we find him?"

"No, this is somebody else. The one who found him."

The other woman said:

"You can explain later."

Then there was a buzzing sound on the line, like when there is no-one at the other end.

Laura wanted to phone her mother, but did not think her number was still the one she remembered. She looked up emergency shelters in Bogotá on the Internet and dialled the number she found, which was called the Hearth & Home Centre. They asked her how old the boy was. She repeated the question to her guest, and he said he was six and a half. From the Centre they said that if he was that old he was *too different* from the ones who had escaped that day. There was no-one else missing. Laura added that the boy seemed to come from the lowlands. They told her she would have to wait until Monday and then give her *report* to the National Family Welfare Institute, which was closed at the weekend for *stock-taking*.

Laura left the boy in the living room and looked for the greyhound to give him his colic medicine. She found Brus trembling under the bed in her bedroom. She told him there were no burglars in the apartment. He was almost cured of his colic. It occurred to her that possibly the boy was a product of her imagination, but when she went back into the living room she found him fast asleep on the sofa. As this was rather narrow, she was afraid he might fall off in the night and hit his head, become frightened, think he had woken in a nightmare, run out into the road and be run over by the rubbish truck that came past at dawn. She picked him up, laid him on the floor, took off his flip-flops, arranged a pillow under his head and covered him with the blanket she had earlier wrapped round his shoulders. She pulled it up over his eyes, as if she were covering a canary's cage. She went back to her bedroom, got into bed and opened *Moby-Dick* at page four, where she had left it the previous afternoon on the bus. She read for a few minutes, but the whale did not appear.

4

The morning after the night Fidel arrived went by very slowly, and would take thousands of words to describe. Better to explain how it functioned. Laura was beginning to feel something that might have been tenderness. The feeling arose slowly, grew and grew until, as it reached the end of time, it burst, leaving behind a bubble of foam that gradually vanished. Then another wave appeared that was identical to the previous one, creating the opposite feeling but made of the same stuff. That was how time passed that morning, as if on a seashore.

At first light, Laura left her bedroom. The boy had turned on his side, and she lay down on the floor beside him. She thought she would have to let his hair grow so that she could comb it with her fingers. She was happy the boy was there. She wished there were other homes like hers in the world outside and more people like her. This wish lost its strength and warmth, and then Laura wished that there was nobody outside, and that the world did not exist.

At times she felt annoyed, at others somewhat disgusted. It felt as if her apartment was pressing in on her. She felt she was drowning. *Not so much drowning as suffocating.* She pulled the blanket off the boy's feet, and saw a small wound on his heel. She called Brus to come and lick it, but Brus did not appear. She told herself that she had just entered the second half of her life. *Where my life is delivered.* A child had come to find her and she felt chosen, with something to do, certain that from now on she would proceed from action to action. At the same time she felt sure that the day had arrived when she could have endless rest.

She also wondered whether the boy had come to her to die, but he was only asleep, and woke up around noon. He asked for some bread, but there wasn't any left. It was a coincidence there had been some the night before, because Laura did not like bread. She felt she wanted to explain what she thought about bread and other man-made products, but she also felt like telling him a lie.

She gave the boy scrambled eggs with rice. He picked the plate up from the table and was about to put it on the floor next to the dog's bowl, but as soon as he saw that Laura placed hers on the table, he put his own back. Laura saw she would have to go and buy him more food. She thought: *If he goes with me, I'll lose him.*

"You're to stay here and wait for me without turning anything on or opening anything," she told him.

"I'm not scared," he said, "as long as he doesn't stay."

Laura took Brus with her in the car. She went to the Olímpica. She filled two bags of shopping and was going to drive home when it occurred to her she would prefer to leave the bags in the car and go for a walk. The woman watching the car park was not outside the supermarket: she never came on Sundays. It was a lovely afternoon, one of those days in Bogotá when the sky is blue and black striped with ochre and seems to offer every kind of weather.

She walked along 95th Street until she came to 9th Avenue, headed south and reached 82nd Street. She left the dog tied to a lamp post and went into La Ganga to buy things she thought she needed: a bar of chocolate, sticks of chewing gum, rubber boots, pyjamas, a sweatshirt, a Batman costume, two pairs of trousers, dungarees, four T-shirts, a waterproof, socks, underpants, a cap and the book *Platero y yo*. Then she went into a pharmacy to buy bath bubbles, a small toothbrush, a comb – which was useless, because the boy's hair was shorter than the tooth of any comb – some little bars of soap shaped like T.V. characters, fluoride toothpaste, glitter shampoo and a towel with a hood that was for children younger than the one back at her apartment but cost almost nothing on purchases of more than a hundred thousand pesos. She also bought herself some lipstick.

She took a taxi back with Brus, because the packages were too heavy to carry. At the Olímpica she recovered her car, and when she got home left almost everything in the boot because she was ashamed at having spent so much. She took out the food, the sweatshirt, the boots and the chewing gum, which she wanted to give to the boy to warn him not to swallow it, so that she could teach him something.

She found him seated at the table. She made spaghetti with tomato sauce. He said he had never eaten spaghetti before. He asked if the dog had, and if there was spaghetti made from other things.

"From other things?" Laura said.

"Like tails," he said, and she saw he was trying to shock her.

5

On the night between Sunday and Monday her guest did not sleep on the floor but in Laura's bed. She slept alongside him, with the dog at their feet. Laura woke up when she heard the word *Brus*. It was the first time anyone apart from her had used the dog's real name, and she decided to ask the boy if he wanted her not to do the same for him, as he hadn't told her what he was called.

"I'll tell you my name," the boy said. "I'm called Elvis Fider."

Laura got him to repeat the second name and confirmed that it ended with *r*. She thought that *Elvis* was too grand, and that *Fider* sounded like an infinitive in Spanish, and so for a while she went on calling him *Hey you*. She had no idea when she decided to call him Fidel.

His family names were Loreto Membrives. The boy added this, looking down and very cautiously. To Laura they sounded increasingly nice as she repeated them to herself and then dialled the Family Welfare number to ask what she should do. But before phoning there she called the old couple whose house she cleaned three times a week. She wanted to tell them she wouldn't be going to work that day. The old lady answered the telephone and, without having planned it, Laura added that she would not be back *any other day either.* She suffered from colic, and it was becoming harder for her to make sure each time that everything was just as she had left it.

Fearing they would think it was not true and that she was only saying it to show off, in her call to the Family Welfare she did not say the boy child had appeared on her doorstep. She said she had found him in the street. The Welfare demanded they both appear at their headquarters *as soon as the distance permitted,* as required by law.

The journey from the apartment to the city centre, where the institution was based, took in half the city. Fidel and Laura went by bus because Laura had never learned how to get there in her car. Fidel asked her to tell him if she saw someone important out of the window:

"The president or anyone else."

She took out the bar of chocolate she had bought the day before and offered it to him, but did not look out of the window.

In the Welfare she waited two hours before she said goodbye to Fidel: one hour with him, waiting for him to be called for what the receptionist termed *the welcome interview*, and the second on her own, while he was being interviewed. In the first hour she told the boy that the animals she most wanted to see were whales, which were so big that people and even houses could fit inside them. She would find them out in the open sea. First she would see a fountain shooting up to the sky in the distance, making the face of the water happy. This was because whales blew through holes they had on the very top of their bodies, through a nose called the spiracle. Then she would see them arch their backs and bring their bulk to the surface, surging and turning in the air, leaping up and then falling back, unleashing a storm. She wanted to see if they shot straight down to the depths and, before disappearing in the world of water, where they were weightless and spent their time singing, whether they waved their caudal fins, that is, their tail fins, which was like saying goodbye. She wanted to know if seeing them for real was very different from seeing them in photographs or on television. Above all, she wanted to see their eyes. The encounter with an animal did not count unless you met that animal's eye. If you could get a glimpse of one of their eyes then you could say you had seen the entire animal, even if that was all you had seen. If, on the other hand, you had seen all the animal's body but not its eye, then you could not say anything. She also told the child that more than once in the history of mankind it had happened that when a whale's back emerged from the water a sailor had mistaken one for an island. The sailor disembarked on it and only realised he had landed on something alive when the island sank or began to move. Some of these sailors lived for many days full of hope after being marooned on a whale.

Fidel listened closely, staring into her eyes when she looked into his, and when she did not, looking towards where he thought she was looking. He said he had never heard about whales before. He asked whether Laura was the only one who knew about them, or whether she and her mamá knew about them, or if everybody talked about them.

The Welfare receptionist told them that in order to save time the institution's psychologist would be carrying out the interview with the aid of another boy:

"A child like our little friend here, but with a house and everything. Well, not necessarily everything."

To justify the delay, she explained that the children they brought in to help with the interviews studied in a nearby school, and that they had to wait until they had a break to go and fetch them. They were of all ages, from six to eighteen. They asked questions that they themselves made up in their

Civics class. Taking part in the interviews entitled them to a bonus that helped raise their marks.

Eventually the female psychologist and the interview boy appeared. They took Fidel down a corridor, and the three of them disappeared behind a glass door at the far end. During the next hour, Laura read a page of *Moby-Dick*.

That morning, Fidel had put on the sweatshirt and the rubber boots she had given him the previous evening. He came out of the interview and back down the corridor with his hands in his waistband and his thumbs stuck between hat and the elastic, as if he was a man who wore a belt and was sticking his fingers in it rather than at the bottom of an apple-green sweatshirt.

Behind him came the other boy and the psychologist. Laura asked what she should do next, and the psychologist told her that Elvis would have to wait until *the placement committee* came round and saw him. They would decide on his transfer to an *intermediary centre*, but she could leave whenever she wished. Laura asked if she could stay until the placement committee came. The psychologist said no, she could not stay that long.

"Well, I have to go anyway," Laura said, explaining that she had a dog at home who must be getting desperate because he had not been out all morning.

"A sighthound," Fidel said. "Brus."

She had taught him the name of the breed in the bus.

"If you'd like to stay here a minute before you leave, señora, while I make a call I need to make. When I've finished I'll come and tell you quickly what we talked about with the boy," the psychologist said.

The schoolboy went back with Fidel to the room with the glass door. The psychologist went out into the street and came back a few minutes later. She told Laura that Elvis had not said much. He had said that at some point before Laura found him he had been made to share a bed with another child.

"He said it was a cot, but he must have been mistaken, because he's too big to sleep in a cot, and he wouldn't remember if he did so when he was the right age for it."

"Did you find out where he came from?"

"No. We asked him if his house was in Bogotá, but he said it was not. Later, when we were checking if he could recognise colours or was colour-blind, he said that from where he lived he could see a traffic light. We could not discover what streets he was referring to. We asked if the weather there was hot or cold, and he said it was both. We asked if he had a mamá, and he said of course. If he had a papá, and he said everybody had one. He did not say their names."

"Could he recognise colours?"

"Yes. Where did you find him?"

"Outside the supermarket, where there are people begging. In the Olímpica on 90-something street . . . 97th Street, isn't it, up above 11th Avenue?"

"I don't know. I haven't had the pleasure of visiting the districts in the north of the city. Was he on his own?"

"Yes. Where I'm talking about there are lots of people during the day, but not so many at the weekend. I found him on Saturday evening."

"What were you doing in the street when you found him?"

They went on chatting a while longer. The psychologist said Elvis had laughed out loud at some of the questions she had asked.

"He has a really nice laugh. As if he was being tickled."

Laura could not remember him laughing with her, but she said yes, he had a really nice laugh.

They could see the two boys through the glass door, standing opposite one another. Fidel was a head shorter than the schoolboy. He talked at the same time as him and waved his hands about. When they came out they seemed happy, or high-spirited, or at least the schoolboy did.

"Alright Elvis, the lady here wants to say goodbye," the psychologist said.

Fidel lowered his head the way children sometimes do when they are expecting to be kissed, so that if they cannot avoid it, it will at least land on their hair.

Laura gave him the sticks of chewing gum she had bought the day before. She told him not to swallow them and to offer one to his friend.

fuck you

2

6

Laura called the Family Welfare to enquire after Fidel. The operator asked her to hold the line for a moment and a recorded message came on while she was waiting. First there was a message of thanks *to our sponsors, the companies that have generously set up grants for the orphans, who are the future of our country.* Then came the sponsors' adverts. Laura had already heard both of them. The one from El Cairo Juices was the same slogan taxi companies played when somebody telephoned to call a taxi. The other one, El Canario Furniture, had her own voice on it. She had recorded it more than twenty years earlier for an advertising agency, and was surprised to hear it still being used.

The operator cut in to ask Laura if she was sure the name she had given was the same registered for the previous day's *session.* He asked if she had signed the *registration and hand-over form,* and she said no.

"Could you repeat the name?" the operator asked.

"Elvis Fider Loreto Membrives."

"How do you write that?"

"Elephant, lemur, viper, iguana, sloth, fox, ibex, donkey, earthworm, rat, lion, orang-utan, rattlesnake, earwig, tapir, octopus, mantis . . ."

"Alright, alright. And yours?"

Laura spelt it without animals.

"If it's been more than twenty-four hours since the hand-over, the placement committee will have assigned the minor to a private itinerant shelter," the operator said.

Laura wanted to know if someone could tell her how Elvis was.

"How he is in what sense? What we offer minors here is initial assistance and an entrance interview. That's all I can tell you. If you would care to leave your number, I can pass it on to the staff for them to ascertain the information and pass it on to you."

Laura was busy with Brus' colic, which she suffered from herself at times – not because he had given it to her, but because it was passed down on her mother's side of the family. It was not until Thursday that she realised three days had gone by and no-one had called her from the Welfare. So she rang again. The operator said the child might or might not be on their register, but if she was not *a relative to the third degree or a duly registered guardian* she was not authorised to *subscribe to the archives.*

On Friday, Brus' colic worsened, which led Laura to remember her mother's family. One of them worked as an interpreter for foreigners who wanted to adopt children, and so possibly had got to know someone in an institution involved with orphans who might have access to information about Fidel. Laura had recently learned about her relative's job at a lunch for the family salt mine that all the heirs attended to receive their five-year bonus.

At the lunch they had been served a soup in which the maize had fermented. No-one but Laura had realised this. The interpreter served herself two platefuls and told them about a trip she had just made to Europe:

We stayed everywhere in the homes of parents who have adopted children here in Colombia through me. They are adorable people, always so grateful, and in their countries hospitality is sacred. The place we liked most of all was Antwerp, it's divine, unbelievable. Yes, good but we didn't spend the night there because there was no family that I'd translated for. In Spain we went to a town that is where the Regueros came from – they are my father's ancestors. It's an ancient Roman name. It used to be written "Regerus" and meant "too powerful kings". It's in Castilla-Léon, because there are two regions named after castles: Castilla-Léon, which is the original one, and Castilla-La Mancha, which is where Don Quixote came from. Then we went to Sweden. You can say the Swedes are arrogant and whatever else you like, but they've earned their place in heaven by taking those children who here would be begging at traffic lights. The little ones they adopt look exactly like the maids we have in Colombia, but they're called Hildegard or something like that. They wear beautiful clothes as if they were in a fairy tale and go to school with all the others in coats and caps and gloves, on sleighs, but that's in winter and when we went it was summer. Their winter is awful, it lasts six months and the day is only two hours long and lots of people commit suicide. By the time winter is over only half of them are left. In spring you go to telephone a friend you had and no, she's not there, she killed herself and the government took back her house, because she had no children to inherit it. That's because apparently the suicide rate is not so much due to the dark winter but because of that, because they can't have children. That's why some of them come over here to adopt. Those Swedish people are so strange. You can't understand a thing. In restaurants you point to the menu, O.K., bring me this, and they serve you something you haven't the faintest idea what it is. No, that's not really true. They all learn English at school. That's why I'm employed when they come here, to translate from English to Spanish and Spanish to English for them. There were two children in the house where we stayed, because their parents adopted a little duo, and they went with us on our outings. They were very well behaved, and asked how you said this, that and the other in Spanish. They were not originally brother and sister. I thought to myself: Won't they end up getting engaged? We didn't go to Italy because we already knew it.

Laura thought of trying to find her mother and ask for her relative's number, but instead she found the Reguero family in the telephone directory. Her relative was pleased that she was concerned about the fate of a needy child. Without asking anything more than what Laura was able to tell her, she passed on the details of one of her god-daughters, a hard-working Law student who was well connected and very friendly. She was doing work experience in the Ministry for Childhood and Youth and would *without a doubt* be able to point her in the right direction.

All that this intern could tell Laura on the telephone was that if she wanted to take the child she would have to present a request to the Abandoned Children Inspectorate. Laura said she did not want to take him, simply to find out where he was and if they were treating him well. She wanted to ask someone about him, in case there was nobody else asking. The intern said that discovering the whereabouts of a missing child was not impossible, but it was difficult. That it required *persistent research* and *knocking on many doors.* She asked for two hundred thousand pesos for her trouble. Laura handed the money over at the door to her building in an Olímpica bag that was too big to hold just ten banknotes.

"That's fine, Doña Laura," the intern said when she had received the payment, "and let me tell you, you haven't changed a bit since the days you used to delight us on our screens. Don't worry, I promise I'll find the child for you."

Possibly in order to commend Laura to her, the relative had said she was an actress, and had neglected to add that the only acting she had ever done was to use her voice for the furniture adverts. Or it may have been that the intern was making fun of her on her own account.

7

Laura tried several times to call and ask how the investigation into what had happened to Fidel was progressing, but the intern never answered the phone. She heard nothing more from her until one day, months after she had given her the task, she received an envelope in the mail with an official stamp from the Ministry for Childhood and Youth. By then Fidel must have had his seventh birthday. She had not been able to read a single further line of *Moby-Dick*.

The envelope contained a fifteen-page document, plus a title page that read: *Report on the Minor Elvis Fider Loreto Membrives.* The paper was crinkly, as if it had got wet and been dried. On the tenth page there was a semi-circular stain from a coffee cup. On the last three pages, the dot over each of the "i"s had been made into a circle with the same blue ink. Some were bigger than others. A few had lines coming out of them to represent the sun. Others had petals drawn round them. Most of them had hair; one also had a hat.

The report had been typed in double spacing, probably to make room for the doodles round the "i"s. The first paragraph read: *At the kind request of Señora Laura T. Romero Sus, we will proceed to document the identity and whereabouts of the minor Elvis Fider Loreto Membrives.* Immediately afterwards came the *First Part*, which consisted of a letter addressed to a certain María Angélica, whom the intern was asking for help in her investigation. Again either making the mistake or trying to be funny, she told her that Laura had been a well-known actress, and requested that the recipient of the letter pursue *this matter on behalf of someone who, as you know, is a woman who dwells in the hearts of all Colombians for the unforgettable roles she has played.*

The intern began her letter by saying that *following exhaustive research into all available data* she had been able to establish that the first contact between Elvis Fider Loreto Membrives and *Doña Laura* had been through Facebook. Apparently Elvis, *a child like so many others, presumably in a state of great distress*, wrote to Laura *searching for protection, aid and warmth* because he recalled having seen her take part in the children's television show "Treasure Haunt" and concluded that she felt *empathy towards little ones.* And that, with the excuse that he needed her address to send a sculpture of her he had made from bottle tops, he asked Laura for it.

Which she innocently gave him. That *on the night of May 7 of the current year* he appeared *bathed in tears and crying his heart out* in the doorway of the building where she lived, and immediately told her that his mother beat him, *because she was jealous of him,* and had taken him out of school to work selling food on the streets despite the fact that he was one of the four hundred best students there.

The intern affirmed that, *according to my reconstruction of events,* Laura refused to go on listening to *the little one,* to which he responded by threatening that if she did not let him go up to her apartment he would hold his breath until he died. He also threatened to kick *the lady's infirm dog, called Bruce* [sic], but she persisted in her refusal and turned her back on him. At that, *the boy appealed to the authorities.* He went to a police station and *made highly damaging allegations.*

According to the intern, it was noted in the police files that Elvis had claimed to be Laura's *natural* son. He said he was aged eighteen, and that if he looked younger it was because he had been hungry all his life. That he had *emerged from his mother's womb* and been at her side for two months, until she *lost him without meaning to.* That he had been found by some people who lived in a place called Bosa and *did not form a family but were a gang or some other kind of group.* That he had grown up as one of them, but *in the knowledge that he was a foundling*. That recently, when he came of age, he had found a *sack buried and well hidden* containing *press cuttings from long ago* which reported that the *celebrated* Laura Romero had lost a baby in the café at the Bogotá International Centre, a few yards from the Conquistador Hotel. The actress had been seated at a table, and had left the baby in his pram next to her so that she could read a book called *Moby-Dick*. When she looked up after reading for an undetermined length of time, she saw that the pram was empty. From the articles he found, Elvis had concluded he was that baby. He added to the *forces of order* that the newspapers did not offer any *substantial reward* to whoever found the missing boy, which seemed to him *confusing*.

According to what the intern said the police said, Elvis ended his statement by affirming that he was anxious to meet his mother again *after so many years*, and that was why he had searched for her on the Internet. That for fear she would not believe he was her lost son he had not revealed his true identity to her either on Facebook or when he went to her home, but had invented the excuse of the sculpture and had said he was simply one of the fans of the "Treasure Haunt" television programme. That his *greatest wish* was for them to meet and become friends rather than to recognise that they were mother and child.

The intern reported that the police *considered the story improbable and fantastic* as the *witness offered no proof of his relationship, not even the said press cuttings,* and because *as was obvious and despite his way of speaking,* he could be no more than nine years old. However, the police then questioned Doña Laura Romero, who denied all the claims made by the *witness* and maintained that she had never had a child, only a dog. The police asked *the lady* if she wanted to take out a *restraining order* on Elvis Fider Loreto Membrives or to lodge a complaint, to which she replied *yes to the restraining order, but no to the complaint, as the boy had not stolen anything.* After that, *the minor* went his way, and nothing more was known of him.

The intern ended her letter by telling María Angélica that despite the restraining order, *now Doña Laura needs to know the boy's circumstances for her peace of mind and because of her feminine sensibility, which leads her to be concerned about the fate of all children in a difficult situation, and also to be sure that Elvis Fider was not going round trying to deceive others and doing to them what he had failed to do to her.* She ended by writing: *I have devoted my best efforts to finding him, but without success. Please help me: you know so many people and so many things and are much better at researching than I am.*

While Laura was reading through all this, the sheets of

paper fluttered as if caught by the wind. This was because her hands were trembling as though plunged into freezing air. Laura felt her colic returning; there was a deep hole inside her which was the only place she could hide from the voices emerging from the papers. *I paid for them to frighten me*, she said to herself, and then wondered whether what she had read was a joke, an accusation or a threat. Whether it was the intern's idea, or if her relative was involved as well. Who was this María Angélica? Was she a real person, or a fiction created by the author of the letter? *What about my mother? Does she know anything about this?* She imagined the writer laughing as she made up this stuff, enjoying herself, but also imagined she had flung it down in a rage, as revenge for something she herself could not remember. *What can I have done to her? What can I have done to whom?*

She put the sheets of paper on the table and tried to control her trembling by taking slow, deep breaths, imagining that the freezing wind that before had seemed to be disturbing the pages of the report had stopped blowing and that all that was left was the air she was breathing, warming up inside her and then rising and being exhaled. After a few minutes she could go on to the next page. She felt ashamed of the curiosity the report had aroused in her, which was not a curiosity to see what had happened to Fidel. She wanted to stop herself reading on, but saw that was not going to be possible.

The *Second Part* of the report was the reply from María Angélica to the intern. It was entitled *Results and Something Extra* and began with a salvo of recondite epithets. The writer proclaimed that she was pleased her *loving and painstaking* work had allowed her to *approach an awareness of the possible whereabouts and identities of the young person under the protection of our morning star, our natural lady, pious neighbour and leading light, the haven towards which we all flock, the gate we all wait before, in whom for not only the children of today, but also for generation upon generation of we adults who were once children, we are blessed to have a rose bush of beauty, a gentle intercessor, a wellspring of sweetness.*

After consulting the *most reliable censuses for information concerning minors reported as missing in Colombia in recent times*, María Angélica had *unfortunately* not found any Elvis Fider Loreto Membrives. So then, *in an attempt at approximation*, she had decided *to extract from the censuses* those children for whom no precise location had been found *on the illustrious date* – this was how she referred to the day when, according to the intern, Laura had said that Elvis had appeared at her door. From among these *candidates* she had eliminated *those who did not coincide in size or features with Elvis Fider*, who, from the description Laura had given the intern, was *small with big eyes.* She had then proceeded *to choose those children whose name sounded similar to the person we are looking for. Then I carried out a selection among the shortlistees. I designed a questionnaire and developed a statistical profile until I could reduce the list to five individuals plus an extra bonus that might seem rather random, among whom Doña Laura may find the person she is searching for.* The intern added that in the *résumés* she was about to list, she had omitted *the most scandalous details of the lives of these unfortunate children, so as not to perturb our gracious lady.*

These were the six shortlistees:

Juan Ismael Loreño Manrique. Born March 2001. Bow-legged when he walks. Says that his dream when he grows up is to be "an animal doctor as well as a Formula 1 driver". Born in Engativá Hospital, and soon afterwards handed to a research institute, from where he was abducted by an atypical gang. Rescued a month later, he was sent to the Argos Foundation, a refuge linked to the Family Welfare, in Bogotá. On May 1, 2011, following a smell, he escaped from the communal dormitory. He says he smelled something was burning with talcum powders and wanted to know what it could be that smelled so delicious. He remembers then begging in one of the northern neighbourhoods, but does not know exactly where, because he "had become drunk on the smell". Says they gave him a little money and a tamale. Returned to the Argos Foundation on May 16. Still there at present.

Fidel Acebo. Born, according to him, in Cartagena on May 15, 2003. His birth certificate has not been found. Lived in the village of La Yenca, Bolívar Department, until his family disappeared in the wake of a paramilitary attack on October 4, 2007. Following this he moved in with alias Gloria, a fugitive from justice, in the city of Barranquilla. In October 2010 was taken in by the regional office of Family Welfare in Atlantic Department. Between then and June 2011 attempted to escape three times. Not known whether between May 7 and 9, 2011 he was in Bogotá. Says he doesn't think he went to the capital looking for Gloria, but did go twice to Medellín, where "there is a casino". Currently held in the Jardín Reform School, Barrancabermeja.

Elvin Estupiñán. Born in Nobsá, Boyacá, on December 20, 2000. Skin covered in freckles, but these are unnoticeable when he becomes tanned. Hair: light brown. Eyes: green with amber flecks. Mother died giving birth. Lived with a great-aunt until his paternal grandfather claimed him following the death of his father, whom the boy never knew, in a water-skiing accident. Grandfather took him to Bogotá and enrolled him in an expensive school. Elvin says he didn't like going to school because his classmates teased him for coming from a small town and nicknamed him "Indian" and "diarrhoea robot". On his grandfather's death in December 2011, returned to Boyacá to live with his great-aunt. Probable that between May 7 and 9, 2011 he could have spent the night anywhere, as he sometimes does this without anyone realising until the third day. Currently in his home or nearby.

Moisés Romero. Born in Guarne, Antioquia, on November 2, 1997. On April 28, 2011 deported to Colombia after being found as stowaway on a Continental Airlines plane headed for New York. Returned to his mother's house on May 10 after spending ten days in the D.A.S. security headquarters. Currently on holiday in Ladrilleros.

Carlos Calixto Vera Nembrives. Mother abducted in the jungles of south-eastern Colombia where she conceived and gave birth, in September 2005. From his birth to six years old, when he was found by members of the Colombian army, Carlos had elevens [sic] *different names and lived in a hundred and sixteen places. The ransom paid by his mother's husband was 34,000,000 pesos. Currently well and living with his mother and presumed father.*

Laura Beltrán. Born 2 May, 2011, died 3 May, 2011. Remains are in the cemetery for newborn babies in Satelite XXVI, in a niche with the inscription: "There is no-one who is not forgotten."

María Angélica, or whoever had written the report, had

gone too far in ending it with the extra bonus of this last candidate who, in addition to being a girl, died the day before Laura had stated that Elvis appeared. Laura tried to think of an adequate description for the intentions of the person who had invented these children and sent her the report in an envelope. *Is it cruelty?* Somebody did not want her to find Elvis and so had tried to lose him in this swathe of missing children. *Perhaps it's not cruelty but disbelief.* The intern did not think Fidel existed, and had simply filled fifteen pages with nonsense in return for ten banknotes. *I hope she spends that money quickly*, Laura thought, and realised she did not understand what her wish meant. Then she opened her mouth and declared that the day she had received the report did not exist: *I swear that this pack of lies never arrived. May the day when it was written be extinguished in dark night.*

In the end, however, she did not fulfil her promise to forget the report, or maintain her curse. She felt the need to visualise those scarred, invented children and succeeded in imagining them one by one, gathered in a house with no walls, in a kitchen, seated and telling the story of their new, brief lives. Maybe they had been born and were alive. Or others exactly the same were alive, and she could conjure them up if she tried. The house where they were had a roof of reeds and a sandy floor, and outside there was a downpour.

Instead of throwing the report in the bin, she put it away in a dark corner of the cutlery drawer, where she kept the shopping list she had made the day she thought the woman who watched the cars was offering her a child.

8

It rained for a week in Bogotá. The drains overflowed and rubbish cascaded down the streets with nowhere to go. The water on the ground was the kind of purple people called grey and in which all the colours of the detritus had combined. Laura was still trying to make headway with *Moby-Dick.* She imagined herself calling the intern to take her to task over the report, and the intern explaining what she had meant. But then Laura realised that the noise of the rainstorm would make it hard to hear their voices on the telephone, and so renewed her vow to forget the whole episode.

After the weather cleared, the puddles lasted another week. Then they dried out and left the city tinged a greyish purple. By the time the mud turned to dust and was carried away by the wind, Laura had decided the intern must have drowned in the deluge.

She resolved to try and find Fidel through the official channels. She found out from the offices of the Abandoned

Children Inspectorate what the procedure was for someone trying to discover what had happened to an abandoned child. She filed a request and filled in a form. It had been ten months since she had had any news of the boy, and the inspector asked her why she had waited so long to apply if she was so keen on finding him. She said she had been looking for him ever since the day she had lost him. The official asked if she wanted it recorded that she intended to claim the boy if in fact he was *available.* Laura said no, that she only wanted to know how he was getting on, and if possible to see him. The official asked her to write a statement describing Elvis in detail and explaining the circumstances that led to her becoming separated from him.

Laura described his face, including the parts that did not seem relevant, not including for example the eyes or nose or mouth. Using the comparison with several vegetables, she described the green of the sweatshirt he was wearing the day she handed him over. She mentioned the receptionist, the schoolboy and the psychologist, who on the day of the interview she had seen wearing a ring with two diamonds on her middle finger.

Almost five months later, at the end of July – which had always been an auspicious month for her – they finally gave her permission to visit the real Elvis Fider Loreto Membrives in the hostel he had been assigned to, the Hearth & Home Centre. Laura had not forgotten that this was the place she had called first to ask what to do with Fidel the night he had appeared in her life.

They met in the presence of the Centre's deputy director. Laura came with Brus, who showed no sign of recognising their former guest. Fidel had grown. His eyes were smaller, and his legs longer. He was good-looking, lanky. His face was starting to acquire the contradictory weight that makes faces look as though they are pointing at the sky. He had begun to grow the nose that suited him, and the nose had begun to make his face look like a boat. He greeted Laura by holding out his hand. She asked him:

"Do you remember?"

"What about Brus?" he said.

"Here he is. Just as old but just the same."

Laura wanted to know if he was going to school. Fidel said that the place he was in was a school as well as a hotel.

"A hotel?"

"But we don't have to pay. We children live here for free."

She asked him if he had many friends. He shook his head and said:

"Of course not."

Laura had not intended to refer to the intern's report. By

now she was sure it was completely misleading and a waste of time, but perhaps she had needed to talk about it to somebody so that she could put it behind her like a dream. Even though she was embarrassed to do so in front of the Centre's deputy director, she could not help asking Fidel if he had lied about her, saying that they knew each other before the night he had come to her house, for example, or that she was his mother, or that they had written to each other on their computers.

"Of course not. My mother is younger."

"But I'm your friend, aren't I?"

The boy said she was, but she was afraid she was not.

Fidel asked why she had not been to see him before. She told him she had looked everywhere for him but been unable to find him. He said the place he was in was easy to find.

"Yes, that's true," Laura said. "I don't know how I did not find you."

She tried hard to stop herself asking why he had gone looking for her *that first day*, but yet again could not avoid it. He answered that he had never gone looking for her. She thought she saw him jerking his eyes in the direction of the deputy director to warn her not to tell his story in front of him, but she could have been mistaken.

"His mamá did this," said Fidel, "but she's dead now. She did everything."

"He means my mother, who was one of the founders of the Centre," the deputy director explained.

Laura told Fidel she had a few things in the boot of her car she had bought for him some time ago, but that by now they probably would not fit him.

"I've grown," he said. "My hair above all. Does it make me look like a girl?"

She said that among the things in her car boot was a towel with a hood.

"But I think it's too babyish for you."

Fidel laughed.

"Could we go out for a while?" Laura asked the deputy director, who had sat on one of the short sides of a desk, whereas she and the boy were sitting on the long sides.

"Where to?" asked Fidel.

"I don't know, to the park perhaps," said Laura. "Where would you like to go?"

"To a barber's so they can cut my hair. I preferred it when it was short."

The deputy director said that for the time being that would not be possible. The next time she came to visit Elvis, which could be as soon as the following Saturday, she should bring a letter making a formal request to take the boy out.

"Normally the minors can go out on Saturdays, provided they are not in the process of being adopted. Elvis is in the *pre-process stage*, so there is no problem for you, *as substitute guardian*, to take him out for a while from time to time."

"I've already been out," said Fidel.

"The outings will have to be on his free Saturdays, that is, every other week, because Elvis is already going out twice a month with the person who was given the pre-process option," said the deputy director. "She is his accredited guardian."

"Does pre-process mean he's going to be adopted?" asked Laura.

"If you wish, you and I can talk later to bring you up to date."

"What time can I come next Saturday?"

"Like today, between eight and nine, the visiting hour, with your letter."

"I've already been out with her three times," Fidel butted in. "With the person."

The deputy director said that Elvis' last outing had been the previous Saturday, and the next one would be the one after. Even though on this Saturday the boy was not going out, visits to the institution could not last more than an hour, which meant that *the current conversation* would soon have to be drawn to a close.

"The last time I spent the night there and they brought me back on the Sunday," Fidel continued.

"And when I come to bring the letter next Saturday, will I be able to see him for a while before he leaves with this other person?" Laura said.

"Yes. If you come between eight and nine, you can have a chat," the deputy director said. "They come to collect him at nine, which is the time he can leave."

She protested, because nine came immediately after eight. The deputy director pointed out her mistake: it was time they were talking about, and between eight and nine there was a full hour, sixty minutes.

Laura surprised herself by asking whether Elvis would be able to sleep over with her between the Saturday and Sunday following the next ones, when it was her turn to take him out, as he had done the previous weekend with the person they had mentioned.

"Not for his first outing," the deputy director replied, "but if everything goes well and you are appointed his substitute guardian, from the second time on you can stipulate his overnighting."

"We'll see each other in a week, Elvis."

"Good," Fidel said, and left the office. From there he either went back to his room or out into the yard to join in the next activity of the abandoned children's daily routine.

The deputy director sat in the seat where the boy had been, across the desk from Laura.

The image of a cage flashed through Laura's mind, although she could not see what was in it. Before the image sharpened, the cage changed to a clean room with white walls and shutters. It would be the same to call it *a white room*, because there would be no reason for anybody hearing it to think it was dirty, but above all the room was clean. In the Centre was an octagonal fountain perfumed with many spices. With the room inside, Laura saw herself walking towards a house with three courtyards that had paintings on every wall. The yards followed on from each other, but each of them fitted the next one inside it. She saw that she could stroll for years and centuries and still discover new animals if she combined the different parts of the already known animals depicted in the murals. She was afraid she was dreaming and made an effort to remain in the part of her mind that was awake.

The deputy director presumed she wanted to know what had happened to Elvis since she handed him over, and told her that the boy had been in the Centre for the past six and a half months. He had been transferred there by the placement committee after spending eight months at the Family Welfare headquarters. He was in the second year, but it was not *really second year* because children of all ages between six and ten had classes together from seven to three o'clock. Elvis was neither the best nor the worst in his class, but, given his previous explanation, that did not mean much. He himself, the deputy director, taught all the subjects apart from Music.

"I don't have the ear for it," he said. "I can't even dance. What about you?"

"No, I don't dance either. But I don't think I have such a bad ear for music."

Like all the other children, Elvis went once a week to a psychotherapist. He was still refusing to give any information about his past. Once he had said that *everybody* had *gone away* and he *had preferred to stay*. He had not mentioned Laura.

The moment came to talk about the woman who wanted to take Elvis in. She was one of the volunteers who visited the Centre at the weekend to give the orphans presents. She was a widow with three grown-up children.

"She has a lot of spare time. She's from a well-known family. I can't remember if her husband was a minister or a representative of... of course, you're foreign too, aren't you?"

"Foreign in what way?"

"Aren't you from another country?"

"No, I'm from here."

"I'm sorry. It's because of the way you speak. I thought you were Spanish or something."

He said this because of the way Laura lisped her "s" sounds, but this was a personal problem, not because she was foreign. The deputy director lowered his voice a little and added, referring to the other woman:

"The fact is, she's extremely rich. The family owns a furniture store and some juices."

"Does she take out several children, or just this one?"

"When her children were small, she used to bring them to play with the ones here. To be frank, she has not exactly mentioned adopting Elvis, but she has given hints. For now, as I said, she has agreed to be his accredited guardian."

"She's trying him out to see?"

"No, how can you think that?"

The lady in question had taken to Elvis because he was *lively* and liked animals. There were two cats in the Centre. Out the back, in the yard. The lady had a farm at El Sisga with rabbits, hens, cocks, a parrot, trout, goats, horses, a donkey and a *famous beehive*.

"El Sisga is a lake, isn't it?" said Laura. "Or a reservoir?

Are you sure they don't want him to work as a farm labourer?"

The deputy director decided she was not being serious and laughed and coughed.

She repeated that she would be back the following week, as if she was scared the possibility might evaporate. She said she was looking forward to visiting Fidel. That she wanted to do so as often as she could. The deputy director said he had something *even better* for her. For an instant, Laura thought he was going to bring her a newborn girl, and could not understand why a baby could seem better to him than this room without children. He got up from his chair, pushed it towards the wall, then stood on it and took down a pile of slender books, announcing as he did so:

"I'm going to tell you how you can become a friend of the Centre."

The way to do it was to buy one of the books, which cost a hundred thousand pesos.

"This is our album. It contains all the children living here. Once you've bought one, you can buy the stickers to fill it with. So it's an ongoing contribution."

On the cover was written "Treasure Haunt". The deputy director passed Laura a copy.

"That's the name of our support programme."

"Like a T.V. programme there once was."

"Like what?"

Laura opened the album and flicked through the pages. The paper was shiny. There were four rectangular spaces on each page where each sticker went. This book had none in it, and unlike other similar albums, for the World Cup or Disney, for example, there were no names printed beneath the spaces.

"Children are adopted and others come in, so if we put names, we'd have to print a new edition every few months," the deputy director explained. "We want only the current ones to appear, those who don't yet have a family. What we do is change the stickers. There are ninety-nine spaces in the book, which is the maximum number the Centre can hold. If at any point we have fewer than ninety-nine, we have to leave spaces blank. You can buy the stickers in this office, in Welfare headquarters, and on the Internet." Unbuttoning his jacket, he took a small envelope out of his inside pocket, and laid it in front of Laura. "Look, open this one." Laura tore the top off and saw it contained six stickers, each with the photo of a child. "Nice to see faces you've never seen, isn't it? Look, they've been taken on a blue background. As if they were at sea."

Laura did not ask with whom or how you swapped stickers you had two of, or whether you did not do that at all. Nor did she find out whether the Centre showed the stickers to potential parents, so that they could choose the child they most liked the look of. She asked if there were easier stickers that were often in the envelopes, and others that were more difficult, and if these corresponded to difficult children, the troublemakers and thieves.

The deputy director laughed and coughed a second time.

"Well, thank you. I'll be back in a week then," Laura said yet again.

"You're not going to leave without an album, are you?"

"I'll buy one next Saturday. I didn't bring any money today. The stickers are called gummies, aren't they? At least, that's what they were called when I used to fill in albums. Don't they call them that anymore? And I wonder why they were called gummies?"

"We call them stickers so that more people will understand," the deputy director said.

"Is there one of him? Can't I buy that on its own?"

The deputy director said that the one of Elvis had already been printed, but there was no way of knowing which envelope it was in, and there was no way one could open the envelopes without purchasing the album.

9

There was a place that Laura had founded years ago. It was an island and a mountain, another world and the far side of the world. In it, neither dead nor alive, just about to say farewell, were all those who had loved her and were no longer with her, those who had departed, those she herself had loved and left behind.

Laura saw that in the future it was possible that one day Fidel would also end up on the island. For reassurance, she told herself that, as he had not begun anywhere, it would be impossible for him to end anywhere. Then she remembered that the island wasn't anywhere either, and concluded it could therefore become the child's country.

She forced herself to send every encouraging thought she had about Fidel there. Shaped like a huge whale, the promise of the boy would swim across the ocean to the other world. When he arrived, it would turn out that in fact he had arrived there before its foundation, and that what looked like an island had always been the whale's body, the surface of its mysterious life. The creature would sink into the waters, dragging the other world to the bottom of the sea, and swim on its way. Only this world would be left, and she and Fidel would stay in it.

On Thursday she looked on the Internet for photographs of whales so that she could study the body that was going to give the lie to the island of her shipwrecks. She wrote descriptions of the photographs on a piece of paper that she put away in the cutlery drawer.

There is an open eye, a hole, made up of concentric circles that look as if they are painted with oil in the water. The eye is the imprint of its vision. It's a version of the body that opens it. All round the white eyelid are small scars. Further out there are deep wrinkles in the skin that reproduce the shores of the eyes in increasingly wider and more distant curves. Do they continue like that until the last one – the last eyelid – meets the coastline?

A whale swims like a sunken ship moving forward from memory. It's an arrow and a wasted effort. Underneath is another smaller one. Unless it is the reflection of the bigger one in the next layer of the sea. If it's not her daughter, growing quietly.

In the depths there is a whale covered with molluscs. Her eye is a black jewel. It is small for her body, but it is not for her body. The whale's eyes are far back in the head. Wherever a whale swims, almost the entire animal arrives first, all the wave, before the eyes do.

Another one is floating in the water beneath her child. The photograph is solid blue. In the world there should not exist any colour apart from this one, unless there exists a good, exact grey.

Another one is swimming vertically, flinging itself towards the land. The land is at the bottom of everything, including the sea. I don't know where its eye is. Is it always on top? On the surface? Is it above the water, so that it can see from the air how its own body is falling? Is the eye the body's child?

A whale has a bubble in its eye that looks like a lens. Its skin is so shiny that it becomes invisible in parts. It seems to be looking at me and downwards. But it does not look at the person looking at it but at something that I'm looking for, and accompanies me. It seems to be pointing out: that is where you have to look, not at me but at the point my eye has strayed towards.

Laura thought it might be good to live and walk with a child alongside her so that she could sometimes tell him where to look. She also thought that with a child days might have the shape of days: they would surge upwards, speed forward, drop down and then disappear beneath the waves once more. Time would be time again. She and the child would pass by, and the world would see them pass by.

On Friday she went for a walk round Santa Ana, the neighbourhood where her former employers lived. On a path by a gully she saw a dead cat that might have been a bad omen. Up above the last houses, the streets converged in a track that rose through the undergrowth and petered out on the edge of a reservoir. Laura could see the city far below. She crossed a viaduct and stood with her back to the high plains, facing the slopes of the Andes, the folds that made the mountain look like the lower part of a huge tree trunk.

Further south she walked down an avenue beside a stream. She had never known whether these streams that ran through Bogotá were channelled ravines or open drains. The muddy brown water flowed sluggishly down.

In the National Park she walked over a big, crumbling concrete map which had a sign that read: "MAP OF THE FOOTPATHS OF COLOMBIA." She trod on the grass growing out of the cracks on the floor painted pale green that represented the valley of the River Cauca.

In the city centre she walked along a road beside a series of rectangular tanks filled with dirty water covered in slime. They were layered like terraces, so that each one flowed into the one below until the lowest flowed underground, perhaps towards the other world.

On her way home she stopped to look at the statue of St

Francis of Assisi on 11th Avenue. As though she were a tourist, she pretended not to be able to guess how long she would remember what she saw. She pretended she did not have all these Bogotá sights engraved in her mind until her dying day. The bronze birds and deer that had once surrounded the saint had been stolen. All that had been left was the wolf, which looked up at him with one paw raised, and an iron structure with two bolts. Brus sniffed the pedestal, and Laura imagined she was taking her dog to live in another city.

10

The car park outside the Hearth & Home Centre was *exclusively for suppliers*, so that on Saturday Laura had to park on the street, two blocks from the entrance. A skinny man was watching the cars. His abdomen was as concave as a spoon. Laura looked in her bag for some coins to give him when she came out, but could not find any. When she turned the corner she saw there was a queue of people waiting outside the Centre's doorway. She thought she could ask the last but one person to keep her place while she went along the line to see if anybody had change to give to the car-minder until it was her turn to go in, but knew she would not do so.

Each child came out onto the pavement to receive their visitor and lead them into the Centre. In front of Laura were a couple who seemed to come from the countryside. The woman was clutching a gift-wrapped package to her chest. From the shape, it must have been a pineapple. Or a *piñata*. Laura could hear the words the country people were saying, but was unable to separate them from each other or understand them. She saw they were looking up and screwing up their eyes so that they could see at a distance, inside the Centre. She imagined all these people had come there because of Fidel, who was a miracle child. The faithful were flocking to him so that he could grant them a wish. They rubbed the tip of his nose while they thought hard about the job they wanted or the person they wanted always to be loved by.

Laura entered the Centre when there were fifteen minutes left before the end of the visiting hour, at a quarter to nine. On her watch one of the hands was on top of the other one, and both were horizontal pointing left, as though holding something or pushing it away, which might have seemed to her as ominous as the dead cat she had seen the day before.

The first thing she did as she shook Fidel's hand was to ask who the others in the queue were.

"People," Fidel said.

She was about to enquire why the orphans were living in the Centre if there were people who knew them so well they went to visit them, but before she did so she realised they were all in the same position as her.

They walked down a corridor lined with doors and went into the room where the children received their adults. There were no windows, and the walls were painted sky blue. In the room were three chairs made of dark wood backed against the wall, a cradle and a couple of dolls' prams.

Laura told Fidel she had brought the letter requesting that he be allowed out with her every second Saturday. Fidel told her to give it to him, and he would hand it to the deputy director, although the director had already given his permission. They did not have time to say much more, because another visitor who had been ahead of Laura in the queue told Fidel someone had arrived to pick him up.

Laura and the boy went out into the street together. A blonde woman wearing dark glasses was waiting at the wheel of a silver Jeep.

"She's the lady," Fidel said. "My guardian. Can you see her?"

Before he climbed into the Jeep, he craned his neck so that Laura could give him a goodbye kiss between his ear and the top of his T-shirt.

There was another woman in the car, who got out to open the rear door for their new passenger. She had a straw hat like a scarecrow's, but instead of wearing it on her head she had it dangling down her back on a ribbon. Her hair was messy, as though she had just got up, and Laura felt that she had seen her somewhere else, close to and often. She was annoyed at not being able to remember where she knew her from: had she known her as a young girl, or when she had already become what she was?

Fidel settled on the rear seat, his knees cradled between the two front ones, and immediately started talking. Laura watched him from the pavement, and it passed through her mind that perhaps they were not talking about her, and that they might be going for an outing to the farm at El Sisga. She told the car-minder she had no change, and promised to give him twice as much the next time.

The following Saturday she parked her car right outside the Centre as she had seen Fidel's guardian do the previous week. She asked a man just coming out if he would do her a favour and go back in to tell the boy Elvis Loreto someone was waiting for him.

In the car, Fidel made a great effort not to ask where they were headed or what they were going to do. She could feel him almost quivering with the strain of holding himself back, and his sense of anticipation stirred her feelings.

"We're going to show you the houses," she told him when they had left the National Park behind. "My houses."

They went to two of them. In both, Fidel asked where *the sighthound* was. Laura repeated that she had left Brus at home because he was not well, and that they would see him another day.

"I've already been here," said Fidel when they entered the first house she wanted to show him. "Yes, I have."

There were two dining rooms, four living rooms, two sitting rooms, two kitchens, and behind the second one, an office. The furniture was rustic colonial, with heavy wooden feet everywhere. Fidel said he had been there with *the lady,* at a girl's first communion celebration.

"This isn't a house, it's a museum," he said. "I was told it was a museum. There are museums of everything."

They walked around it, sat on the chairs, and left.

Laura was slightly worried that Fidel might become confused and think that all the houses she called hers belonged to her, and that she had a huge fortune, or could think that she had been a cleaner in each one, without any of them belonging to her.

Fidel said the houses were like the whales she had told him about. Laura was pleased he had remembered their long ago conversation, but she said no, they were different.

Fidel then wanted to imagine what other thing the houses could be, but she was tired of playing games.

"Games like that aren't always fun," she said.

"With the lady we play at doing ¡Hola!," he said.

"With your guardian? Doing ¡Hola!?"

"The magazine called that."

"What?"

"No, nothing."

At the second house there was nothing more to do, but there were more things to look at. It was the show house of a residential development that had not yet been built. Once it was finished, the house would be the first from left to right if you looked at it from the front and from the outside.

There were ornaments, lamps and tables of all sizes. On one tall round table stood a collection of frames with photographs cut from magazines, one of which might have been ¡Hola!. The bedrooms were on the first floor. One was like a bedroom for a little girl, with pink curtains and bedcover. Another was the parents' bedroom, with a big double bed. Laura's mind drifted. How was it that people had children? Did two become one and make another one so that then each of them would be two again? Or in the end was there only one left?

In the library hearth stood a purple and violet cut-glass flower vase, with two red plastic roses in it.

"What ugly nice flowers," said Fidel.

Laura laughed, and he became more talkative. He told her that in the Centre he had a pair of sneakers and a *cool* shirt that was *tropical with palm trees on it.* And the palm trees were *great*. Then he said that he had a better time with *the lady* and her friends than in the Centre.

"They are *fans* of going to the farm. We are *fans*. They make cheese sandwiches in a press, and they're delicious. They like lots of things, but not others. But there are lots they do like."

Laura thought that if she let him, he could ramble on indefinitely. She said she liked his hair as it was now, longer than when they had first met. Fidel asked if please they could go and get it cut, and she said they did not have time. He said that with any luck the following weekend *the lady* would take him.

All of a sudden the newness of Fidel hit her. She realised how close children were to her own origin. Fidel was talking to her, but he lived in an earlier time, and yet was also further on than her, in a future that she would not see. He was at all the end points.

They had lunch at a pizzeria. He ate spaghetti; she ate nothing. She found it impossible being there with a child, at a table with a candle in the middle: a woman her age with nobody's child.

"We can split," Fidel said.

The straw for his Coca-cola reached up to his forehead.

"Separate?" she said.

Maybe he had an island like hers, another world where he had sent who knows how many people.

"It could also be that I steal you," Laura said. "And do not return you this afternoon."

Before going back to the Centre, she told the boy about the dead bees. She had been woken up by the news on her clock radio that morning. Twenty kinds of bee had died out in the past year. Only a quarter of one North American species was left from the previous January. If the bees went on dying like that, life on earth would come to an end.

II

A fortnight after the bees, when it was her turn to see Fidel again, Laura was woken by the telephone ringing. A woman was calling from the Centre to tell her not to come to collect the boy that morning because she would bring him to her apartment later in the day. The director had authorised the first *overnighting* and had given the woman the task of inspecting what the *reception dwelling* was like. Laura asked her to give a definite time, and the woman said she would be there between four and half past. It was eight o'clock in the evening when they rang the bell. Laura opened the door and they both came in: at first glance and from a distance, Fidel seemed to have shorter hair, but on closer inspection she saw that it was pinned against his head with clips. The woman was wearing an electric-blue silk skirt. She had hitched it up under her arms so that it became a summer frock. Laura thought she must be cold, and remembered Fidel's first night, in his shorts and sleeveless T-shirt. She looked down to see if the woman did not have stockings or shoes on either, but flip-flops like Fidel did when he appeared, but she was wearing some kind of slippers, and she had peacock feathers behind her ears. Laura thought she had seen her before, but was uncertain because so many people had looked familiar to her recently. *Not even in my dreams.*

Her voice rising and falling, like pigeons as they settle for the night on a windowsill, the woman said she was Fidel's *social sentinel.* The sound pigeons make is called *cooing*, but Laura was not sure that was what she had heard now. The sound is also known as *billing*. As for *social sentinel*, Laura imagined it must be the name of a profession linked to orphans.

Without even saying hello, Fidel asked if *this time* they were going to go to the hairdresser's to get his hair cut.

"Tomorrow," Laura said. "It's too late today."

"We couldn't get out any earlier," the sentinel said. "I took him to the navy barber's but by the time we arrived, they were about to close. Now I need to see where the boy is going to sleep so that I can fill in my form and be on my way."

Laura had bought a small bed that folded up into a cube. She had put it in the study and thought she would show it to Fidel as soon as he arrived, but first of all he wanted to show her the camera he had been able to make. It was a cardboard box painted black with a marker pen, with a hole in it covered by a masking-tape flap that could be lifted off. Fidel said he had already taken a photograph with it back at his house. Laura wished he meant by that the Centre and not the lady's house, and that if it had been the latter, the photograph had come out either all white or all black. She asked him what he wanted to photograph. He said a plant, and spotted an anthurium in a clay pot over by the window.

"That one is nice."

"Photographs don't come out at night, Elvis," the sentinel said. "You need sunlight. Besides, there's no paper inside the box. Without that, you can't fix the image."

Fidel uncovered the hole and made as if to photograph the plant: he counted to twenty and then covered the hole again with the masking tape.

"The camera doesn't have any paper in it," the sentinel repeated, slightly irritated.

Laura showed Fidel an orchid she grew near the door onto the balcony. Its petals were a velvety greenish yellow colour, with a blood-red reticle that looked hazy, as if it was behind a veil. She told him that flowers looked like ears and crowns.

"They're nice too, because of the colours," said Fidel, and opened his camera shutter once more.

The orchids seemed to contain a thought, only one thought among all of them.

"Even if there was sunlight and paper," the sentinel said, "the photograph wouldn't come out in colour."

Laura took her to the study, which was now the guest-room, so that she could see where Fidel was going to sleep and then leave. She demonstrated how the new bed unfolded and how, when it was closed up again, there was enough room to sit at the desk. She got a sleeping bag out of the wardrobe and unrolled it.

"It's well designed," the sentinel said, getting ready to leave as she had announced. Before she crossed the threshold, Laura called out from behind:

"Have you seen me before? Do we know each other?"

"O.K.," said the other woman without turning round, and then went down in the lift.

Laura pointed out to Fidel that he had not said hello to Brus, who had been wagging his tail ever since he saw him arrive. Fidel went over to the dog, stroked his paws, then his ears, patted his sides, kissed him on the muzzle, lifted the flaps of his cheeks to inspect his teeth. He hugged him, let him go so as to get a good look at him, then hugged him again with his eyes closed. Laura was taken aback. She had seen no sign of this kind of fascination in their earlier meetings.

Brus licked the boy and wagged his tail, pleased to be putting on with him the show of close friends reunited after a long separation.

"Let's take a photograph of the three of us," said Fidel.

That was when Laura was sure that he liked her: not because he wanted to be with her in a photograph similar to the ones in the frames in her other house, but because he continued to want to show her he could do something. He wanted to show off, even if it was only taking pretend photographs, so that she would like him as much as he liked her.

After posing for nothing, Laura showed Fidel where everything in the apartment went.

"I remember," he said. "I've seen it all before."

So then she told him it was her voice that told the time on the telephone if you dialled 117. She had been hired to record all the times many years earlier, and they were still there.

Fidel did not understand.

"It's a telephone number people dial to hear what time it is," she said.

"Don't people have watches?"

"Do you have one?"

They dialled the number. Laura put the telephone on speaker so that they could both hear:

It is twenty-five minutes and eighteen seconds past the zero hour. It is twenty-five minutes and thirty seconds past the zero hour.

Instead of *midnight,* she had been told to say *the zero hour.* Between the *twenty* and the *five* there was a pause, and between the *eight* and the *teen.* Laura explained she had not recorded words like twenty-five or eighteen, but numbers up to ten and then every ten. The 117 had spliced them together later on, or did so the moment it received a call.

"No, that wasn't you. It's a lie," Fidel said.

"I bet that at the Centre you've never been to bed so late," she said. "Look: it's the next day already."

They unfolded the bed, but the boy was too excited about being awake to be able to sleep. Laura decided not to stay with him in the study. She felt it was too nerve-wracking to wait at the edge of sleep like that; that before long he would close his eyes and no longer see her, although she was still there. So she left him on his own, and later on he got into her bed. He said he was scared. That the bathroom light was on and he could see a white line underneath the door. Laura calmed him down by telling him there was no-one in the bathroom. He could open the door if he wanted to make sure.

"I'm not scared that nobody is there," he said.

Laura got up to switch off the bathroom light and rejoined him.

The next day, all the hairdressers' were shut. They must be the only business to close on Sundays. In order to convince Fidel that a haircut was not that urgent, Laura told him that with his hair like that he looked like a savage, not a girl.

12

Fidel appeared in the doorway of the Centre with an olive-green canvas bag slung over his shoulder. In one hand he was carrying a cardboard box containing a game of Ludo, and in the other his camera, which he had converted into a treasure chest. In it he kept two milk teeth, a necklace made of macaroni, a rough clay pipe and a Flumo marker pen to colour the box black again in case he wanted to use it as a *camera obscura*. In his bag he had all his clothes, because he was going to stay with Laura for a while.

While waiting for the next fortnightly meeting, she had received a letter notifying her that her *application for guardianship in the form of resource shelter* had been approved. The minor would be in her keeping *from the date indicated on the letter, for an initial period of three months,* at the end of which she was to present herself with him *at the head office of the jurisdiction* in order to carry out *the corresponding declaration* and establish *whatever the outcome might be,* either *a return without prejudice* or *adoption*. Laura tried to remember when she had presented a request for Elvis to stay at her apartment for longer than a night and could not recall any such moment, although she could not exactly trust her memory.

When she received the letter she did not know what to say, but then again she did not have anyone to say it to. She thought she should behave like a mother: she would become part of the world, would appear among other women and demand thanks for the gratitude she would show by bringing somebody up. She would aim to turn the child into a likeable man, a man who was similar to a likeable child. She would watch him grow and create a family of the future. She would bequeath him her share in the salt mine, together with those of her mother and brother, and would give him a family from the past.

She could also be a nanny rather than a mother to Fidel. She could pretend that others had asked her to take care of the boy; for example, the old couple whose house she used to clean while she imagined a much better one.

What would happen if after two days she did not know what to do with the child? And if she wanted to keep him after the three months had passed and she was not permitted to? Anyway, death would arrive soon enough to separate them forever. Would she have to discover after her death, in the other world, on her distant island or in her imaginary houses, what Fidel was doing on the earth?

She could also give up on the boy and allow his memory of her to wither like a seed in the mouth of a living person.

Fidel was sobbing as he came out of the orphanage. The deputy director was hanging on to one arm; the social sentinel had hold of the other. When he saw Laura he tried to cover his face, and broke free from one of them. The other one released his arm to hand him over to Laura, and then the shouting started:

"No! I don't want to live there! I don't want to go to the houses. My mother! St Judas Tadeus! Noah's Ark!"

His shouts were punctuated by his stamping his feet.

In the car, while he was smearing the window with spit and snot, he went on:

"I'm not from there, I am a man! I want to go where the men are!"

Intoxicated with his own performance and exhausted from his sobbing, he threatened:

"You'll see."

Following a hate-filled silence they came to a traffic light. Through the window Fidel told a beggar with only one leg and one arm:

"I'm here because I want to be!"

Laura unpacked his bag on the folding bed. She took out three obviously second-hand changes of clothes, a dried-out pineapple and a Batman costume the same as the one she had bought him the first Sunday but had not given him. She asked who Saint Judas Tadeus was, what Noah's Ark had to do with it, and if the costume included a mask.

"Don't make fun of me!" Fidel screeched.

"It's only for three months, Fidel. In three months I'll drop you back at the Centre. I thought you would want to come. We had such a great time with the camera!"

The rest of that Saturday Fidel alternated between scowling and coming out with ideas that had occurred to him: that eating carrots gave you amoebas. That China was Africa. That the Spanish language was for the poor. That Bogotá was going to be destroyed in an earthquake in October because a priest had laid a curse on it centuries ago.

"I'm no idiot," he said when Laura tried to contradict him.

Laura had no idea, because nobody had told her, what had become of *the lady*, Fidel's guardian; whether in the end she had found she did not want the orphan, or that she did want him but it had seemed to her she had had him long enough. All at once, as if the idea had suddenly struck her again, she asked Fidel if the social sentinel was the lady's friend. And if by any chance she was the woman with her in the Jeep the other day.

"She had a straw hat – do you know who I'm talking about?"

"The sentinel is the lady," Fidel muttered. And the one driving the car, *the one with yellow hair*, was a friend.

Laura asked him why he had been shouting for his mother when he left the Centre. If possibly she was somewhere. Instead of responding to that, he answered a question from a long while before. He said that the people queuing outside the Centre to visit the children had nothing to do with him.

Laura examined him closely: the texture of his hair that was already shoulder length, his fingernails, where you could imagine you could see faces looking the other way. She felt a need to look for who the boy might look like. Who could he be similar to? She also wanted to find out what it was that his accredited guardian had not liked. Should she try to find her, discuss with her and her blonde friend – or her dark-haired friend, if the boy was not telling the truth and in the end she was the blonde one – ?

"Your ladies never took you to the hairdresser's, did they?" she said. "We'll go tomorrow."

But that night, after putting him to bed, she changed her

mind. Early on Monday, even before the loaded food trucks came in from the countryside to the supermarkets, she took him out to the plains that were so close to Bogotá but where she had never been, having lived her whole life in the mountains. Fidel was sure to like the endless flatlands at least as much as the farm the other woman had refused him in El Sisga.

She woke up happy, as if she were born on another planet, confident that she and the boy would find somewhere they could share. They headed west down 94th Street and then turned south. As day dawned, they passed through the densely crowded poor suburbs; in the curtain-less rooms they could see how electric lights were being switched on, and would soon be switched off as it grew lighter.

"Look at those people, Fidel. They live all together here. In a little while, once we get out into the countryside, it will look as if the world has emptied. Look at the lit windows, and see if anyone goes from one room to another."

The streets became full of buses. Beyond the dips filled with their headlights, hillsides appeared where even more lights were twinkling.

"Can you see how big the city is? It looks as if it could go on forever, doesn't it?"

The day had dawned overcast. By the time the sun shone

through it would be high in the sky, reigning on its own so powerfully they would not be able to look at it.

They reached the limits of Bogotá at the moment when the street lights went off. They entered the tunnel that went through the last rocks of the Andes. Laura felt that Fidel was happy when the open air appeared at the far end: nothing but the arch of the sky on the horizon. On either side of the highway were ravines that made the descent like a bridge.

"We're heading for the flatlands, where the rivers go to grow," she said to the boy.

"Until they flow into the sea," he said. He was seven and knew things, and with that she believed that peace had been sealed between them.

The sky had cleared by the time they reached the lowlands. There was not a single hollow in the earth, and the blue sky surrounded them in white and yellow.

They saw endless meadows, possibly melancholy ones, full of still cattle of every possible cattle colour. They saw egrets on the animals' backs, and in the sky above, medium-sized and small white clouds. Not even at sea had Laura seen a sky as big as this one over the flatlands. Nowhere else could you see clouds so far off, share in such a distant shadow. She was happy to see for the first time, next to a stranger, this horizon.

They walked through a grove of trees. Laura suggested to the boy that he leave the path and go off on his own for a while; she would wait for him. He should push through the foliage until he began to sense beside him someone he had never seen. He walked away thoughtfully and enthusiastically, imagining the things he was learning, and then came back.

For a long while on the highway back into Bogotá the Renault was behind a cattle truck that was straining up the bends on the hills. Laura was stuck behind it, crawling along, because the road was narrow and she did not dare overtake. Night had fallen ages ago. The cattle were travelling packed in towards the city slaughterhouse, and light shone from them. They could see their heads and hoofs through the planks of the truck. They had no idea which head corresponded to which hoofs. Through the darkness and the mist they could not see the contours of the road. With their mortuary light, the cattle guided them up the mountain, until the last smells of the countryside faded away.

"Do you like the land?" Laura said.

Fidel raised his head to push his nose out of the car window. She heard him breathing in and out. How strange he should be called Fidel.

3

13

From the moment he moved into the apartment, Fidel took it upon himself to make sure all the doors were closed, apart from the room he was in, which had to remain open. He spent the whole day going along behind Laura checking the doorknobs as he went. Every so often he patrolled the apartment to make sure that all the spaces were self-contained. There had to be no doorway through which one of these spaces could exhale or slip into another one. And he was not content when he found the doors closed, but had to close them again himself: open them a little way one by one, then slam them shut. Could it be he wanted to hold the doorknobs to touch wood and drive away some fear?

Brus spent the whole time jumping with fright. Whenever the sound of the doors reverberated around the apartment, Laura relived the memory of the silence of the wood. It seemed to her as if the apartment had grown bigger. In every closed room, in the intimacy of its objects, something unimaginable might happen.

She wondered whether Fidel was going to grow, and how she would notice it if he did. Sometimes she thought he had reached an age when he would not do anything he would no longer do in the future. Anything new would simply be the result of the appearance of characters already written inside him, characters she was unaware of.

During the three months he was staying with her, she was responsible for Fidel's education, and she had to use her imagination to find a school where she could enrol him. By the time she began making enquiries, the school year was already a month old. So as not to waste time, she tried to teach the boy chunks of world history, but she couldn't interest him in it. The story of whales, which had at first attracted him, now only made him more anxious.

"I don't get it, I don't get what it would be like to see a whale," he would say, closing his eyes and scratching nervously. "What exactly is a whale? What is it like inside? And outside? Are they all the same?"

A few days after their trip to the plains, Laura gave him his first writing lesson.

"Say your name. Slowly."

"Elvis."

"What about Fidel?"

"O.K., Fidel."

"No, alright, let's do Elvis."

"Elvis, the man of the house."

Fidel copied the letters she drew, and understood he had to pronounce the sound of them all, starting with the "e". He learned to read his name, but then grew anxious the way he did about whales. Did every letter make its own sound, or say it? How did the letters make a sound, when they were there silent on the page? Did they perhaps bang into each other without anyone noticing? Were you supposed to draw them close up to one another, banging into each other so they would produce a sound? What did it mean to read? What did it mean that Elvis was a word? Where was the word *Elvis*?

Laura preferred not to push him, and to let others carry on teaching him to read when he went to school. She did though show him Elvis Presley. She told him who he was and played videos of him singing. She described his house, which she had visited not long before. She said she had been dreaming of going there for years. It was called Graceland, and was in the United States, near a river by the name of the Mississippi.

"What's the name of this house I'm living in?" Fidel said.

"I don't know, it doesn't have one."

"But how is it written?"

"If it doesn't have a name it can't be written."

"How long have you wanted to go there?"

"To Graceland? Many, many years."

"From before when I was born?"

"Yes."

"From when you were seven?"

"No, I was grown up."

Laura told him that in the Graceland house it was as if every room represented a different region of a kingdom. In the Jungle Room, which was the one she would most have liked to have in one of her own houses, there was an artificial waterfall. Elvis had put his parents' room on the ground floor, near the entrance. You were not allowed up to the next floor, which was where he slept when he was still alive. It made you wonder if that floor was the same as it had been when someone was living there, or if it was empty, if it was clean or dirty, or was a secret hotel. If Elvis' body was there, asleep or dead, or there was any trace of him. The tourists went round the house in single file without being asked to, then came out into some galleries where Elvis' costumes were on display: they were like children's onesies. Outside, next to the swimming pool, were the family graves. They had headstones, which were notices that told you the name of the body buried underneath. The houses of living people, on the other hand, had a front door with a number that arranged them in order among all the other houses for the living, but they did not give the name of the bodies that were on the far side of the door. The tourists left soft toys they bought in the Graceland souvenir shops on Elvis' headstone.

Fidel lowered his head and his face took on a serious expression. He asked if he could tell her *something quickly.* He said he was called Elvis after one of his uncles.

"Oh, is that so?" Laura said, believing for a moment that a door into the boy's past had been left open.

"No, it's a lie," Fidel said, and what if he had carried on with the lie and then she had asked him what was on the first floor of Elvis' house and he would not have known what to say.

Laura saw this might be the moment to ask Fidel something about his life, about relatives or songs. But she also realised that in fact she did not want to know anything about him that was not her.

They played games together. They tried to guess what time it was. They made a bet, and then dialled 117 to find out the truth. They had the game of Ludo he had brought from the Centre, and a Christmas crib she kept stored. Although it was still months to Christmas, they took it out and each day put something they found in the apartment in it. They set it up in the living-room hearth, and put everything there: spoons, glasses, the lemon squeezer, the macaroni necklace that Fidel had brought, a fossil, silver foil to make a lake, bits of toilet paper they chewed and moulded into the shape of snowballs, the anthuriums, the orchid, the Ludo counters. Everything was going to visit the newborn Jesus. But each day, after they had added new things, they sat staring at the baby in his manger with nothing to do, and Laura thought it would have been better to leave the crib without the baby and make a game of their interminable wait, or of the baby growing or pray.

14

In Bogotá, new schools left their promotional leaflets next to the tills in the Olímpica, where customers whose children had been expelled from more prestigious institutions could pick them up. Their names suggested faraway, elegant places: Lycée Monaco, Institute of the Loire Valley Chateaux, My Peloponnese Academy, Complete Tuscan School.

According to its leaflet, the Complete Tuscan School offered *an experimental team mindful of the students' stylistic needs and dedicated to the dramatic structure of human life.* It went on to explain that some lives were divided into three acts, *in the classic mode*, whereas others had only one, and still others changed acts *the way they changed underwear.* Any close observer of the *infant constitution* was able to determine which category each child fell into, and *to administrate knowledge accordingly.*

The Complete Tuscan School took in students throughout the year, and was based in three units of the old Los

Héroes shopping centre, at the end of Avenida Caracas and the beginning of the Northern motorway. It was located among several stores selling all kinds of things, but in particular knitwear that was moderately cheap, made from lilac-, turquoise- and salmon-coloured acrylic wool. The school had been founded three years earlier and was expanding as its students moved up through the classes. At that moment it offered first, second and third years. It was run by a couple of supposedly Italian sisters, the Zannini, who took it in turn to teach all the subjects, Music included.

The location of the classes in the shopping mall was *provvisoria* – the leaflet left the word in Italian. At first, the school had been based in a rented house in La Soledad neighbourhood, until the owner died and his heirs decided to demolish their inheritance and construct a building of *lofts.* On the back page of the leaflet were photographs of these lofts, as well as two phone numbers for anyone interested in buying one.

The pedagogical principle behind the school was the dramatic structure of life, but its *guiding spirit* was *admiration for the super-illustrious men* of Tuscany, that *divine region* of Italy. Each year, its activities were placed *beneath the sign* of one of these heroes of the past. The year Fidel enrolled, this was Giotto, a shepherd who centuries before was drawing pictures of his sheep on a stone when a greater painter who happened to be passing by discovered his skill and encouraged him to become a painter like him, according to the leaflet.

Since he was seven, Fidel had to go into the first year. Before enrolling him, Laura took him to see the premises. When they came out, he said that the children most like him were the ones in the third year, who were more numerous. In that year there were eight, in the second year five, and in the first year, only one.

The Complete Tuscan School gave lessons in all the official curriculum subjects, plus an extra subject taught to all three years in conjunction with Physical Education. If Fidel was telling Laura the truth, this special subject was taught in the shopping centre parking lot so that, with no desks in the way, the students could adopt *positions*, which must have been the physical exercises, while they were doing the extra ones, which showed their *creativity*.

"Today we did an exercise with you," the new student told Laura, full of enthusiasm and talk a week after he had started at the school. "We learned about blessings and curses, and we had to bless a person – that's like promising them something, which means seeing in the future that you are giving them a gift. To do that you imagine you're giving that person a dress on which whatever she needs is painted, so that what she needs will become part of the painting and fall from the sky. *Signora* Zannini said: *Who shall we imagine the dress is for?* I said you, and Luis, who is another boy, said that the dress had a garden painted on it so that in the real world a garden would appear for you, the sort where you grow vegetables, so that we wouldn't have to go out every day to buy food, because I told him we spend the whole time at the Olímpica. Then a second-year girl asked how a garden could drop from the sky. After that we did the curses, and you were in that too."

Laura asked him to explain what curses were. He said they were what he had already told her. She said he had not told her anything. What did they want to happen with them? How had they done them?

"The *signora* said they are the same as blessings," said Fidel.

"How can they be the same?"

Laura paid one of the Zannini sisters extra to teach Fidel to read and write while his classmates, who already knew how to read fluently and even silently, were on their break and were going round the shops and the petrol station at Los Héroes. From the third week of school, Laura also began to help him with the reading and writing. She practised with Fidel in the late afternoon, with sheets of paper from the cutlery drawer: the old shopping list, the intern's report, her descriptions of the whale photographs and the leaflets the schools left by the supermarket tills.

The boy paid attention and understood what he was reading, but an hour afterwards he could not remember what was in the text. *The thing is, I have a bad memory*, he would say, changing the subject to talk about his teacher. He showed how she shaped her mouth when she was saying the letter "e", and asked Laura to buy some bottled water to show her how the Italian women drank. One night, after they had finished eating and Laura had begun to watch a television programme, he stood between her and the screen.

"Laura, there's something I have to ask you, and you have to tell me."

He wanted to know how many boyfriends she had had, or if she had never had any, and whether she had married them, and why she had not had any children with them, and if they had themselves had children, and what the school where the children studied was like.

Laura did not know how to talk about the island she had in another world, the dark mountain she had created and peopled with distant people from the past. It was a place without hope, but it was at the far end of despair. It could be said it was a sweet land, although in reality there was nothing to say about it. No-one who had gone there had ever come back. It was an empty island, even though it was full of people. There were only people, nothing else. It was in the past, but at the same time in the future. It was the centre of the sea. She could talk to Elvis about love and dissolution, about how everything came to an end and nothing was lost, or she could go through a list of names. Anyway, all he was interested in was the chance to hear himself say he was in love with his teacher.

"When I get married," he said, "I think I'd prefer the *signora* to you."

With that he set off on his patrol of the apartment to make sure all the doors were properly shut. When he had finished and returned, Laura told him she had never thought he wanted to marry her.

"I know," he said. "Not everybody can get married to everybody. That's why I said it."

Then he asked if they could be brother and sister, like the two Zanninis.

His obsession with the teacher lessened as Christmas drew nearer. In the Complete Tuscan School this was brought forward to the end of October. As preparation for Advent, the students had to spend half an hour contemplating a print of Giotto's *Nativity*.

Laura commented that what the print showed was the

same as the crib they had made in the living room at home, but Fidel insisted that what the painting showed was not the same as what was in their hearth. The birth in the crib took place in another country, but the one in the painting had happened a long time ago. He said there were angels in the painting. The people had gold round their heads. The mushrooms did not reach the shepherds' knees as they did in their crib, in fact there were no mushrooms, and the sheep weren't as small as the people's eyes. In the painting, the mother was lying down and looked tired after having the baby, but in the crib she was sitting up. Laura reminded him that the bits of toilet paper they had scattered over the fields of Bethlehem were not sheep but snowflakes, the eternal snows of the highest peaks. Fidel said that in the painting no snow was falling, and that was all there was to it, but he did concede that:

"What is the same is that the two children have a good memory and remember everything. They remember even when they were born. That's why they appear as babies, in that shape."

The topic of Christmas naturally led on to that of birthdays, now that Fidel was turning eight. He said he had never heard of turning years. What did she mean by *turning*? Laura reminded him how sure he was of being six and a half on the night of their first meeting, but he did not remember having had any years before seven, and insisted she explain the custom people had of celebrating the date of their birth.

Laura thought it might be good for the year to have a day to celebrate the birth of her child. She suggested they have a party. Even though she had already decided that Fidel had come into the world while she was buying bread on a bus at the start of May, she chose a date in November, the month they were in.

The moment they finished writing the invitation for Luis Palomeque, Fidel's only classmate, and the only person invited, the floodgates of unhappiness opened. Fidel burst into tears and could not explain why. He cried bitterly almost every day until his birthday. He cried streams of tears that ran down inside his T-shirt and must have made puddles in his navel. Laura could not make out what he was muttering in the midst of his sighs whenever she asked what was wrong. *Why did you say you're as sad as a toad?* She asked him if perhaps he was sad because he didn't want a party. He said no, they should have the party, but his torment continued. Brus' ears smelled of salt, of sweating child, and Laura realised Fidel was using them to dry his eyes, consoling himself with the dog or plunging himself even deeper into despair in his company.

15

The birthday party took place one Sunday, and was attended by Fidel, Luis, Brus and Laura. They bought a beach tent in La Ganga and had a picnic in the grounds of the Modern Gymnasium, which was a pleasant school in Bogotá with trees and grass, not like the Complete Tuscan School.

They pitched the tent on a rise next to the football pitch, pointing towards the block housing the school swimming pool. They played with a football and a ball for dogs. Laura gave Fidel a resounding kiss for his birthday, which might have embarrassed him in front of his classmate. She stroked his hair, the cut of which was now a closed matter, and loved him as much as she could, as though she could love herself endlessly. Brus was happy as well, chasing the ball and hunting blackbirds or rolling in the grass to get covered in the smell of the sparrows' droppings. Their guest, however, was sullen. Laura thought she could tell, each time he kicked the football, that he wished he were kicking Fidel, Brus and her.

They sang "Happy Birthday" and ate cake. Fidel asked Laura to tell them a story. She thought a story might improve Luis' mood, and told them two. The first was called "Great Expectations".

> In a village in the lowlands near Bogotá, there was once a poor boy who was the same age as Fidel. One night, on Christmas Eve, the boy went to the outskirts of his village to visit the graveyard where his parents were buried, and got the fright of his life when he came across a huge man dragging a chain. The man ordered him to find a saw to cut off the chain and to bring it to the graveyard. As the boy was walking back to the village, he ran into some policemen who asked him if he had seen an escaped convict. Terrified, the boy said no, he hadn't seen anything. The following night he returned with the saw and some food for the convict, who was still hiding among the headstones. A few days later, the rich lady of the village sent the boy an invitation to come to her mansion and play with her adopted daughter. The mansion was very old and tumbledown, surrounded by an overgrown garden. The old lady was wearing an

ancient bridal gown that she had worn ever since she was jilted and was so moth-eaten it fell apart at the slightest breeze. The little girl who lived with her was very pretty and very haughty, and the boy fell for her as soon as he saw her. Every Sunday he went to play with her and to submit to her cruel whims. The years went by, and one fine day the lady sent the girl to study in Bogotá. Shortly afterwards, a man came to see the orphaned boy and told him that someone, he could not say who, wanted to pay for his studies and to make a gentleman of him. The lad went to Bogotá, completed a degree, and became a doctor. Years later, he met his childhood love once more. She had become an elegant, admired great lady, who treated men harshly as she had been taught to do by the woman who had brought her up. Around the same time, the orphan, who had always believed his benefactor to be the lady who owned the mansion, now discovered that his sponsor was the grateful convict he had helped escape as a boy. He was stupefied, ashamed that this was the source of his good fortune. Shortly afterwards the convict died in a shipwreck, and the shameless young woman discovered she was his daughter. But even though they had the same origin, the boy and girl could not remain together. It was too late.

Luis and Fidel listened in silence, or did not listen, and when the story had finished whispered something to each other and pointed towards the swimming pool. Then Luis said he had only understood part of the story. That the rest was very complicated. Did Laura know another one? Although she suspected he wanted to keep her busy so he would have time to think of things that only concerned him and Fidel, she told them the second story, which was called "Wolf Man".

Once upon a time there was a boy in Russia. His father and mother had married young and lived happily together, although the father often felt desperate and the mother had stomach illnesses. One day when he was a year and a half old, the boy caught malaria. He woke up with a fever, and saw his parents embracing. He had a nursemaid whom he adored and who had lost a son, and a sister who was two years older than him, was very intelligent, and did whatever she liked. The father often took the children to see the sheepdogs and the flocks of

> sheep. When the boy was three and a half, his parents hired an English governess who quarrelled with his nursemaid and called her a witch. Shortly afterwards, the boy started behaving badly. When he was an adult, he thought he had begun to behave badly one Christmas when he didn't receive the double present he deserved because it was also his birthday. At the age of four he dreamt he was lying in his bed, feet facing the window, when all of a sudden the window blew open and he could see that six or seven wolves were sitting in the walnut tree outside the house, staring at him. They were white, and had foxes' tails. They did not do anything: they looked like dogs and did not frighten him.

Laura sensed that neither of them was listening, and stopped. Maybe she was not telling the tale properly. Luis asked if all the stories she knew took place at Christmas. That if what they were celebrating was Christmas and not his school friend's birthday. If that was the case, why didn't they celebrate his as well, which had been the previous month? Evening was drawing in, so Laura sent them to pick up all the leftovers from the picnic. Between them they fed the bits to Brus and the blackbirds, then dismantled the tent.

Laura had promised Fidel that for his birthday she would teach him to cook. She wanted to prepare a special rice dish and needed to buy some things to give it a bit of colour: peas, carrots, peppers, colouring. Fidel and Luis begged her not to make them go with her to the supermarket. They wanted to play and they didn't have long before Luis' mother came to fetch him.

Laura agreed to leave Brus to look after the boys and went on foot to the Olímpica. As she hurried along, she thought about walking: one step led to another, the same but on the other side, which went beyond the first one, which almost immediately caught up, coming from the past and also from the future. The steps always lagged behind. She received and took a step, then another, and so on until she reached a place from where she could no longer see her balcony. She carried on walking, continuously adding up the steps effortlessly, until all at once she felt a shudder, a loosening. It happened in her stomach, in the centre, and although she felt it now, she knew it was the echo of something that had happened in another time.

She turned the final corner to the supermarket. She thought the sensation had passed, that she would soon take out the shopping list and return to the tasks of the present, when suddenly she thought she realised what had shaken her. *My abandonment is unfathomable. It is limitless and bottomless.* She had left two boys on their own, whose mothers she did not know, in an apartment whose owners, builders and previous occupants she knew nothing about either.

The area outside the Olímpica was empty. On Sunday the woman who watched the cars was not there, and nor were the men selling pirated videos or the displaced person from the war who sold bin bags. Laura tried to reassure herself by saying that she had left Fidel on his own in the apartment once right at the start and nothing bad had happened. But as if from a badly tuned radio, she received a message that the boys were not playing. *They're doing a job, they're working.* She tried to imagine what kind of work that might be, and the first thing she came up with was that Fidel and his guest had moved her home *a long way from where the apartment was an apartment.* She ran all the way home without buying anything.

There was only one boy in the apartment. The doors were open in a way they had not been since no-one but Laura was living there. Kneeling on her bed with his back to the bedroom door, Fidel was talking to Brus, holding his front paws up in the air.

"Outside the mansion they tie up a German shepherd,"

he was telling him, "who is a wolf sitting in a tree. When you see him you're going to be so scared that you will run off terrified and you're going to forget the way. Are you going to see him?"

Laura called Fidel by his name. He did not hear. He was having difficulty talking, like someone with his eyes closed reciting an incantation he had not properly learned. She walked round the bed until she could look him in the face, and at once saw he had changed. It was as if his face had slammed shut. His talk to Brus went on for several more minutes. The boy was accusing him of being *a sleepwalking dog.* He said that he ate, slept, went for walks, licked and wagged his tail while *he was in a sleeping state.* That his ears were fake. That the collar he was wearing was made from his sister's skin, *a murdered bitch* whose innards Laura had eaten *and the years went by.* That Laura loved him, Brus, more than she did Fidel, and yet would end up eating him as well. That his dead sister was *Laura's soul in torment.* That he, Brus, was *three times as old* as Laura said. That one human year was the same as seven dog years. That Fidel and not Brus was *the original dog.* That Brus had been thrown into the garbage by his mother and that was why he had ended up in this house changed into an animal. That Fidel had come to save him. That his dead sister had turned into a pigeon, *one of those pigeons in the squares that are missing a claw on each foot and have their feathers brushed the wrong way, their chests puffed up and their heads folded on them, and call whoo-whoo.* That the *real father* of all of them, the sister, Brus and Fidel, was made from a *pile of birds heaped together in a jar and stirred.*

Laura withdrew to the doorway and turned the door-knob, thinking that a sound other than a voice might be better to warn the boy he was not alone. He opened his eyes and turned round. With his eyes open, his face seemed even more tightly shut.

Laura shouted at him, asking why he was doing what he was doing. What was he doing to Brus?

"He doesn't mind," Fidel said, who had recovered his normal tone of voice. "Dogs don't understand."

"Why were you saying *Fidel* if you were talking about yourself? Say *I*. What were you saying? Why were you talking that way?"

"I didn't want him to understand."

They both fell silent until Fidel said:

"I beg you to be so good as to clear something up for me: does he bite?"

That distant, almost comical *I beg you to be so good as to* made Laura's head spin. She took the boy by the shoulders and shook him. Then she let go of him and clung to the dog.

Brus growled softly, or rather did not growl but made that sound between his muzzle and throat that some dogs make when they feel protected.

"Can you hear that noise?" Fidel said.

At first Laura thought he was referring to Brus' gurgling, but then she saw Fidel's eyes were turned up and realised it wasn't that. It seemed to her that his question, when there was no sound to be heard, even if it was said quietly and although night had not yet fallen, came from the same source as *I beg you to be so good as to clear something up for me*, from the same wickedness.

"Be quiet, be quiet, listen," Fidel said faintly. "Luis' mother came to pick him up, but he wants to come back here. He says if he does, he can help us look after the apartment, to clean, and he'll teach us to concentrate. Because we never do that, do we?"

Laura overcame her fear and pressed her lips to the boy's forehead. It was burning. She put him under a freezing cold shower, gave him an aspirin and lay down beside him. At around eight, he woke up. The fever had gone. They went into the kitchen and prepared plain boiled rice.

16

Laura had read somewhere that the fear of ghosts was a fear of numbers: that people will remain and every single one of them continue, all those that have ever been. She had read that ghosts existed and also that they did not, that nobody left any trace behind. She recalled having heard that you could pass through a ghost like through mist, but not whether you could travel from one place to another through a ghost. She had heard of apparitions at country crossroads. There were ghosts within ghosts: cities, ghost ships. Two living people sitting at a table holding hands could summon a ghost to speak to them. Ghosts were like photos taken by Fidel's cardboard camera, printed on nothing. They had the features of those they were representing, but had no air inside them and therefore did not breathe either: they were characters that did not bring the sky with them. She had not read anywhere whether people could have a ghost or not while they were alive, nor if the ghost belonged as a possession to the person it was said to have been, or if it was like an attribute, or if it belonged to them like a child. Laura did not know if your ghost could look like somebody else, nor how long a person took to find out that what they saw or who they were talking to – or the person they thought was their reflection – was a ghost. She did not understand very much about it, and realised anyway that neither what she had learned nor what she wondered about would be of any use to discover if what had possessed Fidel on the night of his birthday was a ghost or something else.

Hours after the rice, the boy called out to her from his bed. He asked if *this* was a dream or reality, and if witches existed. She asked him if he had been having a nightmare. He said not a nightmare. That he had dreamt that he was very sleepy and in his dream he could not fall asleep. Laura took the chance of reading him a page of *Moby-Dick* she had not yet reached, and he asked if the sea really existed. He stayed on his own in his room, but later on came into hers to say he had been staring at some shapes on the floor, *diamonds or squares.*

"Two were dead, and one was about to disappear."

Early the next day, as they were walking towards the school bus stop, Laura told Fidel he was eight now; that this was his first day as an eight-year-old. He looked at her seriously, with a look that was different from all the looks he had given her before, but which to Laura seemed more appropriate than any other he had given her. It was somewhere between resignation and a warning, as if he was convinced that both of them were making a mistake. Laura even thought that perhaps it was not Monday but Sunday and they had got up early for no reason because it was not a school day, although their mistake was different, and this was not the moment to find out what it was.

Every night of the following week was painful and confused, as if linked to empty days from elsewhere. Asleep, but with no sleep in his voice, sometimes lying on his back and at other times standing up, Fidel repeated each night what he had said the previous one, always adding something new. On the third night counting from his birthday, he first mentioned Beauty Parlour Two. He said he had been there. He asked if he was lost or not. Laura thought he was able to recount his dream while he was living it, and wondered if it could be said that dreams are lived. She believed she was witnessing the manifestation of a gift.

On the fourth night, Fidel said he was in the beauty parlour, but they were still calling him to go there. He said that in the parlour – although he did not say *the parlour* but *Parlour* like a proper noun – that in Parlour there was *a place further inside* but he could not *find the hole.* Each morning he got up and went to school as he did every day, with no memory of the phantoms of the previous night.

And that was how it was every night until there were seven in total.

Laura had heard that you should not wake up someone who was sleepwalking, but not what happened if you did. Did the sleepwalker go crazy, get angry? During his trances she tried to talk to Fidel, mixing the waking world with the sleeping state he gave glimpses of, so as not to demolish him with a sudden awakening. The third time he was in Beauty Parlour Two, she told him to try to remember that he wasn't there but in the apartment. He said no, he had *fallen* there, and described the parlour in detail: how big it was, the smell, the sound of footsteps, some locks of hair that a broom with green bristles swept under a rug, the combs on the dressing table in front of the mirror, *some basins where heads were washed, a bed where they pulled out leg hair,* dry head massage, *jojoba oil and honey almond and shampoo for fine hair.* Clients were lining up outside to get in. In the queue were human beings and animals. Each of them was carrying a gift-wrapped fruit to give to a friend they met inside. Some of the animals were soft toys. Others had a head on the tip of their tail.

"No such place exists," Laura told him, reminding him what his bedroom was like, with a bed that folded up into a cube, his desk, and Brus.

No longer worried about waking him, she almost shouted, desperate to bring him back, for him to remember *the day*. That he had lived in the day, all day, wide awake. He replied that he was also living in *Parlour* and remembered that as well. So then Laura asked him not to carry on remembering. That he simply change places. That he check every corner of the place where he said he was, and he would see she wasn't in any of them. That he look closely at some of the things he was describing and he would see that they weren't really there either. That he see, even if it meant not remembering anything ever again.

"Yes, it's true you're not here," he said, "but now Parlour is full of people like Laura. Are they your family?"

Laura told him to close his eyes in Parlour just as he had them closed in the apartment, and with his eyes shut look towards the next morning. He would see what happened every day and would also happen in the future: the walk to the stop, the bus, the school in the shopping centre, his teacher's face, the board, the desk, Giotto.

"At the desk there are two ladies," Fidel said. "They're looking at a hand."

He was talking, Laura thought, about the table for *manicures.*

According to him, he spent the following night hearing about Laura. He gave her summaries of the comments and stories he heard, but he felt *bad* repeating everything and besides he was worried that *Parlour people* could hear he was talking to her.

"The thing is, I don't know if I'm hidden."

Laura saw she could have been the author of the parlour. Instead of going to the island in the other world where she had deported them, her half-forgotten loves had made a detour towards this other place. Or maybe she herself, without realising it, had dreamt up the island in the image of the place where Fidel was; possibly the island had always been an enchanted house, full of ghosts. But why a beauty parlour? And why were they calling for Fidel? Did they want her to remember them again, to look for them in reality, and tell them what had happened in her life?

"When is it, Fidel? When is it there?" she asked, without knowing what she was hoping to settle with her question.

The boy said nothing, and so she rephrased it:

"At what moment are they there? Are they only in the parlour, or elsewhere as well, like you? How long do they last? What time is it when you go there?"

But Fidel did not respond to any of this.

Laura considered the possibility that the parlour could be full of people whom she would never meet but who, while they were there, knew about her. She thought it more likely it was the same members of her world who were there. Her mother and brother, for example. Also there might be those she had often seen but would never in reality see: kings, queens, actors, actresses, Elvis Presley. Ishmael from *Moby-Dick* could be there. So could those who had fallen silent after having resounded in her past: the blonde girl with a little foreign brother and sister outside the Olímpica, the man selling jam on the bus. Or Fidel's family: his first mother, his father. They all met in that parlour, on that corner, in that chorus, perhaps unaware that they were there while they remained – alive, dead, or asleep – in the spot they really inhabited.

"Could I go and see?" Laura said.

"Of course," Fidel said. "But there's no way in."

One night, Laura thought she had discovered that what had disturbed the boy was her making up his birthday. She was to blame for having given Fidel a birth because she had wanted to give him a future. He had turned round to see who had been expecting his arrival in the world and when he found no-one, had been summoned by all these strangers.

"I know now I'm not hidden."

"How are you?"

"They want to know how you are, Laura. To know what happened to you."

Every so often the boy's jaw clenched and his brow clouded over, and she thought the voices talking to him were exaggerating their stories. On the seventh night of his trances, after reporting what was being said in the other place, Fidel said:

"Something I can't say, I can't say it."

He opened his mouth as wide as he could, as if he wanted to swallow a head. When it was at its widest, in mid-yawn, he also opened his terrified eyes. Then Laura had an inspiration. She ran to the kitchen, picked up the bag of salt and tipped it over his head.

The next night he slept without vistas, but on Sunday he mentioned the parlour for the first time when he was awake. He had gone to his room to do his writing homework while Laura wiped the dining-room table with a cloth. All of a sudden he appeared beside the table. He asked Laura if she knew what Beauty Parlour Two was. He said that was what was written on an illuminated sign that had just flashed on in his head. He did not believe that she did not know. His mind had wandered while he was doing his homework, and the sign had come on and called him. No, it had not called him by his name, neither Elvis Fider nor Fidel, but by his face: over and again it had sent the image to his mind of his own face.

All that this meant, Laura told him, was that he needed a haircut. It was her fault for letting weeks and months go by without taking him to the hairdresser; and that because the visit was postponed so long it had turned into a beauty parlour, which was *the same but more complicated*.

"I don't want them to cut anything," said Fidel, and added that they wanted him in the parlour to introduce him to a girl. She was pretty and nobody else in the world had been found who wanted to meet her. "She is about fifteen, or no, perhaps more, but she still goes to school. She has dark circles under her eyes from not sleeping. She doesn't sleep because she doesn't feel sleepy. The sign in Parlour says I'm going to Russia with her so that she can feel sleepy for the first time. When I have another birthday I'm going to start my life of freedom with her."

17

Laura was helping Fidel do his homework with another painting by Giotto di Bondone.

"They told the Virgin what the future would hold and she heard and then they put a baby in her ear."

"Is that so, Fidel? The strange thing is that in your school they teach the Annunciation when they have already taught about the birth. Did they miscalculate and find they had too much time left before Christmas?"

"No."

"Look at the book she's holding. Write that she was reading and the angel came and interrupted her. Or that the angel lived in the book and she opened the book and disturbed him."

Fidel wrote very slowly in his squared notebook, with a blunt pencil, stumbling over what he was writing.

"He libed in the book and then what?"

"It's 'lived' with a 'v'."

"He li ved in t he book and Mar y sa w hm."

"No, she didn't see. She opened."

". . . ry o pened the bo ok and what?"

"Disturbed him."

"Di sturbd him."

"Write that he is the Angel of Inspiration."

"Hes calld the an gel of in s pi ra . . ."

"With a 't'."

". . . sion."

"No . . . 'tion'. It only sounds like an 's'."

"In spi ra tion."

"That's it."

On Thursday, Fidel stole some things from the supermarket. Back in the apartment, he took the haul from his pockets and laid it on the dining-room table. Laura thought she had to tell him off, while at the same time excusing him because by displaying the objects he had taken without earning or even wanting them (a metal scourer, a pot of oven-cleaner, a bar of clothes softener) he was only trying to resolve the problem of his birth.

On Saturday they went back to the Olímpica. Fidel promised he wouldn't put anything in his pocket. The woman who watched the cars came over saying: *I'll keep an eye on it.* Inside the supermarket, while she was crossing off items on her shopping list, for a moment Laura wished someone would steal her Renault. When she realised what she was thinking, she dismissed the idea, and put it down to tiredness. She came to a sudden halt in the aisle of tinned food. How could she get some rest? She felt she had come up against a serious problem. All her life was going and carrying on going, in an endless and tireless succession. And if there was no rest, how could you say that you were getting tired? Rest did not exist for the living.

As she walked down the frozen-food aisle she again felt as if she suddenly could not breathe, or rather like a stabbing sensation, had a wish that somebody would rob her. She wanted an invisible hand to touch her without knowing who it was touching; she wished that a character would suddenly appear in the tireless succession of her life and affect her, and she would never know who it had been, who had appeared invisibly, for her to imagine who it was when he had already gone. Did the theft point to a door to another world as Fidel's beauty parlour did? *A fake door, a door painted on the wall.*

She saw her car was still in the car park, still belonging to her. As it was switched off and still, perhaps it was resting. Were cars like animals that did not sleep? Did human beings rest when they slept? *At least when you're asleep you're lying down and don't have to hold your head up for a while.*

While Laura was wandering through her thoughts, without her noticing it Fidel was growing angry. The only thing he had said in the supermarket was to ask her to buy potatoes, because *now* fried potatoes were his *favourite treat.* When they reached the car park, he said:

"But I don't like all fried potatoes. The ones they give us in packets at school stink. They're called *chips for jerks.*"

On the drive back he went on and on at Laura, himself and the whole world, and his bad mood lasted all weekend. Whatever he laid his eyes on brought a complaint and led to bouts of swearing. His school notebook was *for fucking mental retards.* The potatoes that Laura fried, *what have they got in them? Rotten phlegm?* His homework: *The Zannini can do it with her tits.* Television was *for lousy bumboys,* and reading was *for sons of bitches and kids born through assholes.*

And what did Laura Romero do? Did she say anything? Did she contradict him? Tell him to stop? Did she find it funny and feel somehow tender towards Fidel's string of foul-mouthed complaints? Did she throw the fries into the rubbish or eat them all herself? What was she waiting for?

On Monday morning she walked with him the two blocks to 7th Avenue and waited for the school bus by the statue to Amerigo Vespucci. Then she took a bus across the city to the south-west. She was going to see Maritza, *clairvoyant, fortune-teller.* Laura had been to see her once before, more than twenty years earlier, in the hope of hearing what she believed another woman would have liked to hear in her place. Possibly Maritza was still living in the same house and was still telling fortunes and could say what was happening to Fidel, and what somebody like him could expect.

The girl who opened the door had the biggest rings round her eyes ever seen, double and triple multicoloured circles, like the ripples from two coins tossed into the dense waters of her eyes, into a pond of water and petrol.

Laura recognised the room where she had sat on that previous occasion. The details had stuck in her memory because, in order to remember the events that Maritza was predicting for her, she had distributed them around the room as she heard them. She had thought it would be easier for her to retain the description of the future if she placed it in these surroundings and recalled them. She had attributed each prediction to a different piece of furniture, to each ornament. Here, only slightly duller than before, was the mirror that stored the announcement the fortune-teller had made that she would have a child. Here was the cushion that represented the death of her brother. What was missing was the chintz sofa covered with plastic sheeting on the left as you went in, where she had placed the prediction that she would do the 117 voice-overs. To the photographs of ectoplasms hanging on the wall, in which she had placed the possible outcomes of a love affair that was bothering her at the time, had been added others of people newly deceased a century earlier, which had no equivalent in the future of her past.

Maritza was sitting by her work table in a dark green velvet armchair that coincided with the prediction of good results from the salt mine. Laura could not have said she had aged. She could not even have said this was the same woman she had met. She had only seen her on that one occasion and it sometimes happened that faces slid in her memory.

Light came in slowly and hazily through veils and screens. The lampshades had fringes and were covered in ordinary-coloured handkerchiefs. Rugs imitating oriental ones filled the entire floor. They probably came from a place even further east than the rugs they copied. Maritza's table was covered by a yellow felt cloth. Laura saw and remembered the metal chair where she had sat twenty years earlier . . .

"Oh, it's you: what a miracle!" Maritza said on seeing her come in. "Have you just dropped by or are you staying? Will you be taking the waters of the *spa*?"

Laura was surprised the woman recognised her. She was probably confusing her with somebody else. Laura thought that talking about a *spa* in a place like this was a joke. She sat down, and Maritza went on:

"Don't worry, I didn't mean it about you *staying*."

"Yes, no."

"Let's get started then. The last time you were here you were afraid you had missed your last chance. Or did you say your *only* chance?"

"That was the first time I came."

Maritza laughed knowingly but with compassion and freedom, and this freedom kindled her curiosity, while her laugh revealed a chipped tooth. Laura thought the clairvoyant wanted to confirm whether her prediction had proved correct and whether her client's former fears had proved groundless. She wasn't sure she could confirm it.

"It's never the last chance," Maritza said, dismissing a sense of pride that had overtaken her curiosity, or giving in to it.

She unrolled an astral chart across the tablecloth. On it were scrawled odd letters that were meant to represent stars. She told Laura to turn her palms upwards above the table, the cloth and the chart.

"You said goodbye to someone, just before you came to see me," she said, touching Laura's hands and staring into her eyes. "There should be someone who loves you more than anything else, and you believe him, even if you think you don't. That's the first thing about you. I can tell by your temperature." Letting go of her hand, she used her first finger to trace a path through the alphabet soup of constellations. Then she followed the same line back, stopping and tapping the centre of the chart. "This is today. This is the crossroads of renewal, the Dove, which is magnificent. Next to her, here there is a spiral, which shows what is to come. That spiral is no longer there. Tomorrow in its place is a great Carp: a great calm. Can you see it? The fish lives in the waters above. It comes from before there were fishes, from when God separated the waters above from those below and created the heavens between them – do you remember? This one is from the waters above. It is a fish, but gives milk. You can't see it without a magnifying glass. Now we are in the Milky Way. We say that this part here in the middle is the sky. Those little dots that look like flies are us, human beings. That's why it's said: *We drop like flies.* In the sky, in the house of the Swallow, I see a woman. Your mother? Lean forward so that I can touch your head. Here there's a little bone sticking out." *Here* meant her occiput. "It doesn't have to be your mother. You've seen her time and again. She wants something that you want. Here she is again, in the Moon. Buried on the Moon. She had something you also had. You carry on walking. There you are, standing on Venus, your hands clasped behind your back. You are obvious, in a double-breasted grey coat, but that could only be seen through a telescope. Now you are passing between Venus and Mars, on your way to the constellation of the Pelican. You have just made a great effort that you think came to nothing. But look up here: it's turned up on Saturn. Just so that you know: what rises to Saturn will last. And here there's a dog, in the constellation of the Dog. It's a dog, nothing more. Give me your head again. The dog is here as well, in the curve," she said, stroking her forehead. "And here –" pointing to the chart again – "in the constellation of the Goats, there's a flock of goats. That means it's possible that in the future you'll move to the countryside. Here's the shepherdess, who is you, and here are the trees. An apple! Look behind you. No, not there. Behind you. You didn't see it: it disappeared down the back of the chair. It was very small, tiny. Everything here is too small to be noticed. That's the problem with this job. Even the present is seen in the distance. Not long ago you had a visit. You'll have another one before long. But the two are the same, and there is another one, because there are three of them. Look, you can see them on the chart, clear as day: the Three Wise Men, who are going to visit you. But that doesn't mean it's them, of course. It simply means some people. They're coming to see something you have: a boy, I think, but I'm not sure, because the boy is visiting you too, isn't he? This circle here is the boy's mouth. What a huge mouth! This boy is all mouth. That means he wants to talk. Ever since he was born he could talk, talk about anything, say his name and say 'Mamma' and everything he comes across. You are crying. He is going to leave you, but he'll come back. Here he is in the Crow. Yes, he is definitely going to return. Who doesn't? And something else: in the future you are going to remember. You will remember many shapes, and many of them will remember you."

Laura wanted to ask her when Fidel would leave, because that had to be Fidel, and how patient she would have to be to see him return, but she said nothing. Out of the table drawer Maritza took some envelopes like those with the stickers from the "Treasure Haunt" album, tore the tops off, shuffled the stickers as if they were a pack of playing cards, fanned them out and held them with their backs to her client. She then went on, as if she had heard the question Laura had not put to her:

"Patience is not a matter of quantity. It has no limits. But *there's no need* for patience." She placed the stickers face down on the table, and concentrating again on the chart, she pressed her index finger on one corner of the paper. "Look, here it says there could be long journeys. This blank space means somewhere that is at the extremes: either very far north or very far south, very high up or very low down. The sky has no top or bottom. It's a white space: possibly a Pole. Or maybe it is you, and that white speck is your head, with time. In the quadrant of those you have known there is a crowd. Here there is a man, under the sign of the Bees: he's neither fair nor dark. He's low on the ground, but has a high voice. He has a great fortune, but more like a king than a rich man. You're not going to meet him, because you already know him. He's there in silhouette and half-length. He must be full-length in the next chart, which is the one for the person who has an appointment with me at ten. Of course, that's it, because the future is that person who is coming after you, isn't it?"

Laura agreed, nodding her head and producing the kind of sound made with the lips pressed together that is like a question: *Mmm?* Maritza said nothing, but kept staring down at the chart. After a minute she said:

"Now tell me what you want me to reveal."

Laura wanted to hear more about the man who was neither fair nor dark. Who could he be like? What star could he be compared to? It had to be Fidel. Eventually she said that she had had a child, just as Maritza had described, and she wanted to know if he would grow up to be an adult.

"He's eight. His name is Fidel. He stood beneath my window and found me. I left him and lost him, looked for him and found him again. I visited him and he visited me. Then they left him for me to look after, and this December they'll tell us if we can stay together. But I'm not sure. In recent days he hasn't seemed the same. Ever since his birthday at the start of the month he has changed. I don't know whether he has grown or what it is."

"I know who that boy is," Maritza interrupted her. "But it's not that he has changed, it's that he is always becoming what he is. Look, here he is, in the corner of the Donkey. He hasn't had his birthday yet this year. The birthday, under the sign of Scorpio, is this other boy. Think, think."

Laura felt disorientated and in her confusion thought she could see the future, the past and what Maritza was suggesting she should think about. The other boy was Fidel's classmate, Luis Palomeque, who on the day of the picnic had said his birthday was in October. If from that day on Fidel was not the same Fidel, it was not because he had changed, but because he *had been* changed. When she had left the two boys on their own in the apartment, they had changed places. Luis had stayed with Brus, and Fidel had left with his friend's mother, or with his own mother, or who knew where, and had not returned.

This is what she more or less suggested to the clairvoyant, who guffawed.

"No, I don't think it's that," she said when she stopped laughing. "How could that happen? The two boys are friends and chat to one another, that's all. Or do you think you could have got confused?"

Embarrassed, Laura said she wasn't being serious. The thing was, the previous days had been so strange, *so awful*, that she could imagine anything. She recounted in detail Fidel's nightmares and his rage.

"I'm scared he's going mad," she concluded, her voice cracking.

"No, of course he isn't," Maritza said, leaning over the table and touching her hair, not to read her head but to stroke it. "All children are like that. They are all full of things, they're like enchanted houses, and not just Fidel. But I must say you can't even imagine what he still has to go through. I don't see this in the chart or in your head, but it's my prophecy: everything is going to happen to him. Literally everything. What a life your boy is going to have!"

Laura asked what she could do for him not to suffer so much.

"Why?" Maritza retorted. "He has to suffer what he has to suffer. What we all have to suffer."

"What if he dies during one of the attacks he gets?"

"Those aren't attacks, my child. They're called transports. Or transitions. Why would he die? All children go through them and yet they go on. But there was no reason you should know that this always happens. You've never had children, have you?"

Laura opened her mouth to declare that yes she had, that she had in fact given birth to this boy who had not come out of her, but in the end didn't say it.

"I mean you didn't have children *before* and no-one told you about them," said the clairvoyant, who read her thoughts. "Although there was no need for you to have a child to know that's how it is, because everyone knows that. Have you never heard somebody who had children talk about it? And wasn't it the same for you as a little girl? It might have happened to you when you were very young, and you don't remember. Didn't you have a younger brother? You told me that the other time, or I told you. Fine. For some children it only lasts one night and it's over. They have a fit of crying or get earache and then it goes. If you ask me whether they get over it entirely, or how long the effects last, I couldn't tell you. Some say they last all our lives, although they gradually diminish; others say they last even longer."

Laura shuddered to think that everyone knew something

she was unaware of, and was disappointed to discover that something she thought was unique to her happened to the whole world. She also felt relieved and grateful. As she listened, her gratitude turned into joy and joy became tranquillity.

Maritza was still talking:

"It was the same with Mari, my daughter. She was the one who opened the door to you – did you notice her? She's twenty already: how time flies! Just imagine, now she's my assistant and is expecting. Around the time she had a baby brother, or rather when I had him, Mari showed all the symptoms. It was just like you told me: stealing from the supermarket, nightmares, and a room full of creatures, although none of them were soft toys like you described, and the place she went to wasn't a beauty parlour but a waiting room. The worst of it was that it lasted almost a year. They say that for some girls it lasts much longer than for boys, and that they even start to bleed. But at any rate it's better to be a girl because they're allowed to be given flowers while they're still alive and can wear them in their hair. When my husband and I saw that the months were going by and Mari was still being transported, we were worried it wasn't that but something else, even though nothing terrible showed up in her stars. We took her to the paediatrician, who sent us to a psychiatrist, who sent us to a neurologist. We tried some regressions that a client recommended, but they had no effect. I had to pick the girl up and put her on my breast, can you imagine? She wasn't allowed to talk because she had to pretend she was a baby. I fed her with a spoon that was supposed to have come from my breast. And we couldn't repeat the same food twice, which meant I soon ran out of ideas and ended up giving her awful mixtures: sardines with vanilla biscuits and Vicks Vapo-Rub. Enough to make you vomit. But she didn't vomit, she didn't even retch, just went on laughing and crying like a baby. We had to teach her right from the start everything she already knew, and since I was so bored and wasn't sure anyway what she did and didn't know, I was a dreadful teacher. Then we tried a treatment called 'reconfiguring the family' that was in vogue and which consists in exchanging the roles played at home. Her father played Mari's role, she took over mine, I was her little brother and he, Felix, who at that time wore a patch over one eye because he had a squint but which later on corrected itself, was his father. Felix, it's true, has not been through it yet as far as I know. Well anyway, that treatment was just as useless. Mari continued with her swearing, breaking things and the need to make friends with invisible enemies. The only thing that worked was time, because it wasn't an illness but what I'm telling you, but now your appointment is at an end."

Laura asked if she could put one more very short question to her.

"I want to ask about my dog, a greyhound. If he's going to last."

"I can't answer for the future of a dog," said the mystic. "Dogs don't show up on the chart. They appear here and there, lying down."

18

At about nine o'clock, for the first time since he had been living with Laura, Fidel locked himself in. At midnight, a loud noise started to come from his room, her former study. Laura did not go and look; she pulled the covers up over her eyes, and the sounds were fainter, like a mouse scratching. Then there was hammering and a scraping sound, and at a certain point a bang. Brus was under the covers with her, and she talked to him to remind herself she wasn't alone. Usually, she only said his names – Beauty, Statue, Flower, Brus – but that night she spoke to him in complete sentences: she told him how much she would love to have a tail like his, and his rapid feet, soft ears, his fine moustaches, the arrow of his muzzle, his dolphin's nose, those eight silky fins, the lofty antlers branching out like oak trees, the hard pads on the tips of his feet, the feathers of a thousand colours, his proud mane, his silent tongue. The dog was calm, not disturbed by the noise. He lived far away, meeting her at every moment, within his own being and always safe and sound.

At dawn the noise ceased. Laura heard Fidel's door open and a moment later the bathroom door close. When she went into the boy's room she saw that all the objects he had collected were multiplied, in pieces: the presents she had given him, and what he had brought from the orphanage. Everything was in tatters. Fidel had cut his clothes into strips. He had transformed them into loops, a bunch of streamers. The toys had been smashed with a hammer and the bits painted black with the marker pen. The yellow bus was marked all over with crosses. The camera was squashed. The Ludo counters had teeth marks in them, and the soft seal toy was striped like a zebra. *Platero y yo* was a heap of blackened pages, and every one of the thousand pieces of the Piazza della Signoria puzzle that Laura had bought to chime in with the Complete Toscano School was covered in ink.

On top of the scrawls, Fidel had poured kitchen oil on all the fragments. He had covered the bed with balls of chewed toilet paper like the ones Laura had taught him to make for the snow in the crib, and he had poured a winter of salt on the floor. She wondered whether he had left the study in the night or if he had stolen the scissors, the hammer, the oil, the salt and the toilet paper, the instruments of the disaster, beforehand. Although she had not slept, she had not heard any doors open. The boy had used at least two rolls of toilet paper and all that was left in the bag of salt to make this new crib. He had used the paper not only for snow, but to wrap round the desk and chair, like Egyptian mummies.

Apart from the snowflakes, the bed was untouched. One corner of the duvet was turned down, and there was a hollow in the pillow. Fidel had found time to sleep after devastating this poor world throughout the night. The sun rose, and he came out wearing one of Laura's T-shirts, a yellow one he must have found in the bathroom. It was like a short tunic on him.

CAROLINA SANÍN is a Colombian author, columnist and academic, born in Bogotá in 1973. She obtained a PhD. in Hispanic Literature at Yale University and has taught at the State University of New York and the University of Los Andes. Her previous works include novels, essays, short stories and writing for children. *The Children* is Sanín's first novel to appear in English.

NICK CAISTOR has translated more than forty books from Spanish, Portuguese and French, including novels by Paulo Coelho and Eduardo Mendoza. He has thrice been awarded the Premio Valle-Inclán for translation from the Spanish.

119

1	2	3	4	5	6	7	8	9	10
11	12	13	14	15	16	17	18	19	20
21	22	23	24	25	26	27	28	29	30
31	32	33	34	35	36	37	38	39	40
41	42	43	44	45	46	47	48	49	50
51	52	53	54	55	56	57	58	59	60
61	62	63	64	65	66	67	68	69	70
71	72	73	74	75	76	77	78	79	80
81	82	83	84	85	86	87	88	89	90
91	92	93	94	95	96	97	98	99	100
101	102	103	104	105	106	107	108	109	110
111	112	113	114	115	116	117	118	119	120
121	122	123	124	125	126	127	128	129	130
131	132	133	134	135	136	137	138	139	140
141	142	143	144	145	146	147	148	149	150
151	152	153	154	155	156	157	158	159	160
161	162	163	164	165	166	167	168	169	170
171	172	173	174	175	176	177	178	179	180
181	182	183	184	185	186	187	188	189	190
191	192	193	194	195	196	197	198	199	200
201	202	203	204	205	206	207	208	209	210
211	212	213	214	215	216	217	218	219	220
221	222	223	224	225	226	227	228	229	230
231	232	233	234	235	236	237	238	239	240
241	242	243	244	245	246	247	248	249	250
251	252	253	254	255	256	257	258	259	260
261	262	263	264	265	266	267	268	269	270
271	272	273	274	275	276	277	278	279	280
281	282	283	284	285	286	287	288	289	290
291	292	293	294	295	296	297	298	299	300
301	302	303	304	305	306	307	308	309	310
311	312	313	314	315	316	317	318	319	320
321	322	323	324	325	326	327	328	329	330
331	332	333	334	335	336	337	338	339	340
341	342	343	344	345	346	347	348	349	350
351	352	353	354	355	356	357	358	359	360
361	362	363	364	365	366	367	368	369	370
371	372	373	374	375	376	377	378	379	380
381	382	383	384	385	386	387	388	389	390
391	392	393	394	395	396	397	398	399	400